THE PRIVATE CLUB

BOOK THREE

J.S. COOPER & HELEN COOPER

CHAPTER ONE

Meg

Present Day

Brandon Hastings stood in the doorway, looking tired and insistent as he spoke. I watched him talking, yet I felt like I was hearing his voice from some sort of distant speaker. His words were tinny and vacant-sounding. It was as if I were having another out-of-body experience. I looked over at Greyson and was surprised to see that he was staring at me and not at Brandon. He had a look of worry and concern in his eyes. And he looked scared.

"Mind your own business, Brandon." Greyson finally turned to look at his friend, and I could see his gorgeous features turn into a grimace as he glared.

"This is my business. It's always been my business." Brandon stepped into the room and sighed. "We shouldn't have let it—"

"Be quiet." Greyson's voice rose and I froze.

"It's over, Greyson." Brandon looked taller and bigger than I remembered as he took a step toward Greyson. I could see Greyson's fists clench, and I felt my heart stop for one brief second. Where they about to fight? "Remember what we said, Greyson? When we first started the club?"

Greyson stood as still as a statue, and silence fell in the room as they stared at each other.

"We said we wouldn't harm anyone." Brandon's voice cracked. "And we failed in that mission."

"Things changed," Greyson finally said. "Life changed."

"Because of us."

"No, because of you."

I looked back and forth at them, wondering if I was finally going to hear the truth. Part of me wanted to know the secrets behind the private club, but another part of me was afraid. What if I heard something that broke me inside? I was falling for Greyson—slowly but surely. My heart had already carved a spot for him. I knew that I wanted more from him than what we had. I wanted to believe in him more than anything, but I was scared.

"If you really believe that it's because of me, then you're more of a fool than I thought," Brandon sighed and ran his hands through his hair.

"I've always known you were a fool." Greyson turned towards me. "Meg, now you can see why I don't listen to Brandon Hastings."

"I told you not to hire her." Brandon looked angry as he spoke. "Meg, you need to leave now."

"Tell me why," I said softly, daring to go against Greyson's wishes. "I want to know why you were insistent that I not work here."

"I'm sure you've realized by now that this isn't a bar." Brandon gave me a wry smile.

"I'm sure you've realized that Meg is an adult. An adult who can make her own decisions." Greyson walked over to me and put his arm around my shoulder. At first I felt protected, but then I realized that his act was more one of possession. His action wasn't to provide me comfort but to tell Brandon to back off.

"Yes, I can." I shrugged my shoulders and stepped away from him. "I want to know what's going on here." My voice cracked as I looked back and forth at the two men. They both looked obstinate and angry. Where one was dark, the other was light, but they both emanated the same energy. I could feel it in the air, the slight buzz of electricity that alerted everyone to the fact that anything could happen in the next few moments.

"We didn't start the club to hurt anyone." Brandon looked at me with pained eyes. "That was never the intention. It was just a bit of fun. A way for us to live the lives we wanted to. We wanted everything to be on our terms. We wanted women on our terms, yes. But we didn't want to use them. We didn't want to gain anything from them."

"What did you gain?" I whispered, barely breathing.

"Nothing." Brandon shook his head. "We gained nothing."

"I suppose it's all my fault." Greyson looked at me with bleak eyes.

"Do you know what grief is, Meg?" Brandon turned towards me. "Do you know what it's like to have your heart snatched out of your body? To have your tears shed tears for your tears? To feel like your life will never be the same again?"

"No." I shook my head and bit my lip. And that was the problem. I'd never really felt. My life had always been so safe. So unfeeling. My parents were just there. My friends were just there. I'd had no great loves. No great heartbreaks. And I felt like I was just coasting in life. I felt like I was just there, barely existing.

"When everything went wrong here …" Brandon sighed. "I felt awful. I felt guilty. I felt uneasy. But I never really felt heartbroken. Not the way I should have. Not the way a human being should. But I realized that was because I'd lost a part of myself. Somewhere along the way, life had become too easy. Women had become too easy. I was coasting on the edge and I didn't care. It wasn't just me. I had Greyson, and if there was anyone more fucked up than me, it was Greyson."

"I'm still here, you know." Greyson rubbed his forehead and stared straight ahead. "I can tell my own story of insularity and detachment."

"It wasn't until I met Katie and lost her that I realized what true pain was. What heartache was. And I knew that I had lost her because of my sins. I didn't deserve her."

"But you're the one who dumped her. You dumped her even though you loved her?" I frowned, feeling uneasy. How would Katie react once she found out that her boyfriend was a monster?

"I dumped her because I loved her. I dumped her because she needed to grow and I needed to make peace with who I was as a man." He looked towards Greyson. "We were wrong, you know."

"Wrong about what?" Greyson frowned.

"Life isn't just about us and about sex and money." Brandon took another step towards Greyson, and as I watched his movements, I finally understood what Katie saw in him. He wasn't just handsome and strong. There was a delicate grace and warmth in his aura that gave him an animal magnetism that was hard to resist. It made you drop your defenses, even if you knew you should back off.

I looked back at Greyson. His body was tense. His eyes were squinted, his breathing uneasy. I could tell that the situation was hard for him. He wasn't in control, and I could sense that a part of him was unraveling, and that gave me hope. An evil man wouldn't be on the brink of unraveling, would he?

"Meg, when Greyson and I started the club, we were—or at least, I was—a different man."

"Do you take advantage of innocent women?" I asked loudly, not able to take it anymore. "I want to know what's going on. I need to know what's happening."

"So do I." The voice was familiar, and I looked toward the door in shock.

"Katie!" I screamed and ran over to her. "Oh, Katie, what are you doing here?" I gave her a big hug and she smiled at me sadly.

"I was worried about you." She squeezed me tightly. "I was worried about you and I kept asking Brandon what was going on." We both turned to look at him, and he stared back at us with a blank expression. I could see Greyson looking back and forth between Brandon and Katie, and his face looked mutinous.

"I'm fine."

"I didn't know." She pointed at Brandon. "You lied to me. You said you were going on a business trip."

"This is the business trip I was talking about." Brandon stepped towards Katie and then stopped abruptly as she threw her hands up. "I didn't lie to you, Katie."

"You knew I was worried about Meg being here." Katie's voice broke. "After everything we've been through, you lied to me again." Katie's voice was angry. "I'm so done with you, Brandon. I can't stand—"

"I asked him not to tell you." Greyson's voice was direct. He looked me over for a few seconds before continuing. "I called him and asked him to come help me take care of a situation."

"What situation?" My voice cracked.

"I asked him to come and get you." Greyson's voice was cold and he avoided eye contact with me. Brandon's face looked surprised, and I felt my body growing cold.

"What?" I took a deep breath. "What do you mean?"

"I asked Brandon to come and take you away. You shouldn't be here."

"You wanted me to be here. You hired me." My voice was a mere whisper in the room. I could see Katie giving me a concerned look, but I couldn't look at her. "I'm still in training."

"You need to leave, Meg." Greyson's face was like stone as he looked at me again. "You've been here too long. It's time for you to leave."

"So you've used me and now it's time to discard me? Is it because I slept with you or because I know the truth about you?"

"Oh, Meg." Katie's words were hushed and worried.

"Yeah, so I'm a fool." I bit my lower lip. "I know that now. I didn't want to believe you could be that man, Greyson."

"I never told you to believe that." He shrugged. "You should all leave now."

"Greyson, no." Brandon shook his head. "You can't—"

"You've changed your life, Brandon. You have real things to lose. You should leave." Greyson walked back to his desk. "You should all leave."

"Greyson, this isn't for you to decide." Brandon looked at Katie and sighed.

"Yes, it is." Greyson picked up a pen. "I'm fine. I have a heart as cold as ice. I'll survive."

"I won't let you treat women like that anymore." I walked over to his desk. "You hear me, Greyson?"

"What are you going to do about it?" He looked up at me with bleak eyes.

"Meg, come on. We should leave." Katie called me over to her, and I turned to look at her with unseeing eyes.

I noticed that she and Brandon were standing together holding hands. Once again, they were reunited—just like that.

I turned away from them to stop the pounding in my heart and the jealousy from seeping through my veins. Why was it so easy for them? We still didn't even know what was going on, yet Katie was quick to believe that Greyson was the evil one.

"What happened to Maria?" I looked at the floor as I spoke. "How did she die?"

There was silence in the room then. I could hear someone's distant footsteps as they walked around the club, and then we all listened as a door closed somewhere. I looked at Greyson then and his blue eyes gazed into mine with an emotion akin to sorrow.

"Which Maria?" Katie's voice was squeaky, and I knew that she was in for a shock.

I spoke up then. "Brandon wasn't engaged to a Maria in college, Katie."

"What?" She sounded confused. "What's she talking about, Brandon?"

"The Maria I told you I dated in college was a lie." His tone was somber. "I was never engaged to a Maria in college."

"But what about all the stories you told me?" Katie frowned. "They were lies?"

"I did date a Maria. And no, not crazy Maria," he sighed. "I only pretended to date her because I promised her father I would look after her."

"Then what fucking Maria did you date?" Katie screeched.

"He dated a girl from the club," Greyson said. "Even though it was against the rules."

Brandon nodded. "I made a mistake."

"What?" Katie rubbed her eyes. "Maria was a girl from the club?"

"She was the girl who changed everything." Greyson jumped up. "She was the girl who changed our lives."

"She turned us from regular guys to the sort of guys you see put on trial for war crimes." Brandon sighed.

"She's the one who made us realize that ..." Greyson paused and looked at me.

"She's the one who made us realize that we were no better than cold-blooded killers." Brandon stared at Katie with sad eyes and I saw her body trembling as she stared back at him. The words from his mouth had been spoken slowly, and each syllable had seemed to cause him pain. It was as if he were reliving the horror that had changed his life.

Katie stood there, frozen. She didn't know what to say or what to think. This changed everything. Suddenly everything she thought she knew had been called in to question. Now she knew that a saint and a sinner could be the same person. I looked at Greyson for a moment and wondered what his truth was. For some reason, I had a feeling that he was all sinner and that the pits of hell were waiting eagerly for him.

CHAPTER TWO

Greyson

24 Years Ago

Two girls stared at me from across the room. One smiled at me with wide, eager eyes. The other one tried the seductive approach. They both played with their hair, and I knew that I could have either of them. I turned away from them and waited for Brandon to enter the room. I was disgusted with their behavior. Not because they weren't allowed to flirt with me. I didn't care about that. They were both fairly attractive. I was disgusted because I knew they were best friends. I saw them everywhere together, giggling and whispering and doing whatever else girls did. Yet they were both trying to attract my attention. Didn't they care that one of them would get hurt if I hooked up with the other one?

"Brandon, here!" I called him over, grinning at him and the box of pizza he had in his hand. "I hope you got pepperoni."

He grinned back at me and slid into the seat next to mine. "Who said you're getting any?"

"Hurry up. I want a slice before Professor Carter gets here."

"You know he'll be ten minutes late as usual." He laughed and handed me a slice. It was deep dish and pepperoni. I grinned as I stuffed a mouthful of pizza into my mouth.

Now this was more like it. Brandon had been my best friend for the last four years, the person I was closest to in the world. I'd never do anything to jeopardize our friendship. I'd definitely never date a girl he was interested in. That's one of the reasons why men were better than women. We cared more about the bro code and keeping our friendships strong. I'd never let sex come between me and Brandon. We were brothers for life.

"You're such a pig." Brandon laughed at me as I grabbed a second slice and chewed it down quickly.

"I was hungry."

"Why didn't you eat before class?"

"Dude, I was too busy planning out the club."

"You're still thinking about starting a club?" Brandon sighed.

I ignored the expression on his face. "It's going to be epic. We're going to have our own world."

"We don't need our own world. This one is hard enough as it is." Brandon pulled out the textbook and started reading. "Now, shh. I need to read real quick."

"What's our motto going to be?"

"Motto? What are we, Boy Scouts?"

"Idiot." I glared at him. "Let me think. What about 'Two boys, one world.'"

"Nope." He shook his head. "Two men, one exam in three hours, which one man is going to fail."

"I studied last night." I winked at him. "But I do like the idea of two men. Two men, one club."

"What about just two men?" Brandon looked up at me thoughtfully. "It's always just going to be us."

"No, it's not." I shook my head.

"I don't mean just us at the club, but just us in charge of the club."

"That's true. Doesn't that sound gay, though? Two men?" I made a face. "You know I love you, but I don't want you, bro."

"You're breaking my heart." Brandon clutched his heart and laughed. "You're full of shit, Greyson. As if you could get a guy like me."

"Eww, you're making me sick." I laughed. "Let's do this again. Two men, one club, infinite women."

"Now that's hot." He grinned. "Infinite women is always nice."

"I thought you were a one-woman man?" I raised an eyebrow at him.

"That was when I was young and dumb."

"That was last year."

"Things have changed." He shrugged and I let it go. Both Brandon and I had changed since high school. Both of our worlds were different now. We never spoke about it, but we both knew we were brothers for life. The only people we could both count on were each other. It was as simple as that.

"Yeah, who needs one woman when you look like us? We'll have women begging to be with us."

"They can beg all they want," Brandon laughed. "They'll be lucky to have one night with me."

"Now that's what I'm talking about."

"One night with the Italian stallion and they won't know what hit them."

"You're not Italian, Brandon."

"I'll be anything I want to be."

"Well, I'm hung like an African." I grinned.

Brandon shook his head at me. "That's so racist."

"It's not racist if it's true."

"Greyson, I'd shut my mouth if I were you. People already think you're a cocky asshole."

"Well, they wouldn't be lying." I jumped up. "I'm the fucking king. I run this shit."

"You're a rap star now?"

"I'm king of the world. We both are—or we could be. Once we start this club, we'll be loved and worshipped. It'll be the most exclusive club in the world."

"You think so?"

"We'll make it that." I paused. "And no one but us will know exactly what's going on."

"How's that possible?"

"We'll think of a way." I sat back down again and thought for a minute before looking at him seriously. "We can't trust anyone, Brandon. This is between us."

"I know." He nodded back at me and smiled. "No matter what happens, it's between us."

"Hey, Greyson. Hey, Brandon." The two girls finally made their way over to us.

"Hey." I nodded without smiling.

"What you guys up to tonight?"

"Fucking one of you?" I looked at them as they giggled and thought I was joking. "Or would you prefer it to be both of you?"

"You're so funny, Greyson!" The blonde giggled again and pushed her chest out. Her blue eyes twinkled as she slowly licked her lips. She was letting me know that she wanted to be the one who got the prize.

"I've heard that before." I nodded in agreement and grinned at Brandon, who was sitting there with big dopey eyes. I wanted to laugh out loud.

He was such a dope. He could talk the talk now, but he'd never really walked the walk, aside from a one-night stand he'd had the day his father had married yet another woman a few months ago.

"You guys can come over tonight if you want. We can have a study date."

"I don't study with girls." I stared at the redhead. "I fuck."

"We try to be accommodating." She grinned at me eagerly and then looked at her friend. I could so fuck both of them. I knew it as surely as I knew that I could get the blonde to go into the men's room and suck me off at that very moment.

"Brandon and I have laundry to do tonight." I yawned and sat back. I could see the surprised look on his face as I blew the girls off.

"Maybe we can help."

"Maybe not." My voice was sharp with irritation. "I'm not interested." I spelled it out to them clearly. Blondie's face fell and the redhead had an evil glint in her eyes as they realized they'd been dismissed, but I didn't care. "So, Brandon, wanna catch a movie later? I'll pay." I heard the girls' sharp inhalations as they walked away and I grinned.

"You just told them you were going to do laundry tonight." Brandon shook his head. "And then you slipped up and asked me to a movie. They most probably think you're a jerk now."

"That wasn't a slip-up." I gave him my 'who do you think you're with?' glance. "That was my don't-swim-in-the-ocean-if-you-don't-like-sharks lesson to them."

"You didn't have to be mean."

"I wasn't being mean. I was being real. They're sluts."

"Greyson!" Brandon hurriedly looked around the room to see if anyone was listening.

"Come on, now. We could have had a foursome tonight and they don't even really know us."

"I'd rather a threesome and you stay in your room." Brandon grinned and I laughed.

"You know it's true."

"Well, they were a bit obvious."

"I don't want those types of girls at the club. Women should know their place."

"What do you mean?"

"All women do is bring men down. Men lose their shit over women. And for what? For some pussy? Gimme a break."

"You've heard of the power of the pussy, bro."

"Only because we give it to them. Everyone knows men run the world. But that's strong men only—weak men crumble." My mind fell to my brother. "Women try to make you love them and then they leave with either your money or your heart."

"Not all women."

"What women do you know who give a shit about you?"

"I dunno." Brandon shrugged, and I slammed my hands on the table.

"Exactly. There's no point trying to lie to ourselves or even go down that road. We can get what we want from women who know the deal."

"What do you mean?"

"I mean, as long as we keep our hearts out of our pants, we're cool."

"So we're going to have girls at the club then?" Brandon said after a few minutes. "What will the girls be doing?"

"Whatever we want them to do." I raised an eyebrow. "There will be no request too big or small."

"So it'll be like a private, no-questions-asked strip club?"

"No." I shook my head. "Strip clubs are sleazy."

"Sex club?" Brandon's eyes widened.

"There will be sex. And plenty of it. But no. It's not just about being a sex club, either. It's not anything we have to define. It's what we want it to be. It's just the private club. No one will really know what goes on there. That will be part of the allure."

"So we're just going to call it The Private Club?"

"Yeah." I nodded. "And only you and I will know what's going on."

"You're fucked up, you know that, Greyson?" Brandon shook his head at me and grabbed his books as the professor came into the room.

"Every single day of my life," I whispered as I pulled out my pen.

I saw the blond girl walk back into the room with a tissue in her hands. She was rubbing the corners of her eyes, and I could see she'd been crying. She avoided eye contact with me, and I stared at the front of the room, trying to ignore the guilt in my heart. *I'm preparing her for the real wolves out there*, I told myself. Better to learn the harsh realities about men now.

The professor started talking, but I couldn't hear what he was saying above the throbbing in my ears. As averse as I was to love, I still didn't want to hurt anyone. That wasn't my goal.

I stared down at my desk and thought back to my life before my mom had died. I thought back to the joy and the laughter and I missed it. But then I remembered the man my father had become since her death and I knew that I couldn't break my vow to myself. I was never going to allow a woman to break me down like my father had been broken.

CHAPTER THREE

Meg

Present Day

"Brandon is not to blame for anything." Greyson's voice was firm. "I was the one who is responsible for what happened and what continues to happen. Ultimately, I make all of the decisions at the club."

"So you're saying that all the shit that goes on here is you?" Katie's face was void of emotion, but I could tell she was hopeful.

"Everything that's gone on here is all me. Brandon didn't even know about it until it was too late."

"Greyson," Brandon spoke, and Greyson shook his head.

"You're right, Brandon. You have a new life now. Leave."

"Let's go, Meg." Katie looked at me. "Let's just go."

"I don't know." I hesitated. "I don't think I should go."

"You don't need this job. Brandon got you fired." She glared at him. "And he'll help you get your job back."

"I don't want my job back."

"Then he'll help you get a job at a new firm."

"I don't want that." I looked at the confusion in her eyes. "I need to see this through."

"See what through?" She sounded mad. "Please, just leave with me."

I shook my head. "I can't do that."

"You should go, Meg." Greyson joined the discussion, and I looked at him with hurt eyes.

"I'm not going anywhere until I find out what happened to Nancy and exactly what's going on here."

"You think you're going to save all these girls?" Greyson's tone sent a chill down my spine. "You think you can—"

"Just tell her, Greyson," Brandon pleaded. "Please, let's just get it out in the open."

"I don't think so." Greyson sat back down. "I want you to leave now."

"You think that I'm just going to leave and—"

"Brandon." Greyson's voice was cold. "This isn't your problem. You and Katie need to leave."

I stood there as a warm feeling spread through me. He hadn't asked for me to leave this time.

"I'm not going without Meg." Katie stood her ground. "There's no way I'm leaving her with this maniac in this place."

"I'll be fine."

"I wouldn't count on that, Meg." It was Greyson's turn to speak up. "I've told you before that I'm no angel."

"I haven't been burned yet."

"You haven't been close enough to the flame."

"I'll take my chances."

"Meg!" Katie chided me. "I get it. He's cute. But please … He is not worth it. I can tell from one glance that he's not a good guy. Please, Meg. Let's go."

"Listen to your friend, little Meggie," Greyson laughed. "She knows what she's talking about."

"What's that supposed to mean?" She glared at him.

"I'm just saying that you should know what it's like to date a dirty dog." He smiled at her sweetly. "Now leave."

"Brandon." Katie frowned. "I want to go now."

"Katie, I'm sorry," Brandon sighed.

"We're not going to talk about this here." Katie gave me one last glance. "Is there anything I can do to convince you to leave?"

I shook my head wordlessly.

"Please don't let sex make you think he likes you, Meg. Sex is nothing for men like him."

I stared at her and felt tears pricking my eyes as she spoke. I knew she was right, of course. But that didn't stop me from hoping that something else would happen.

I stood there wondering why I didn't run out as fast as I could. And then it struck me. I couldn't. My body wouldn't let me leave. A part of me started to understand why women stayed with men they knew were inherently bad. When you were bitten by the love bug, it was hard to do anything but hope and pray that somehow it could work out.

There was silence in the room as we all stood there. Finally, Katie shook her head and walked through the door, Brandon following behind her. He stopped at the door and turned back to face us before looking at Greyson one last time.

"It doesn't have to be this way, Greyson. You don't have to be this way."

"It always had to be this way." Greyson's voice was bleak.

"This isn't over, Greyson. We're not in college any more."

"Just leave, Brandon. Go explain to your woman why you're not the spawn of the devil before it's too late."

"Call us, Meg. If anything happens, call us." Brandon glanced at me and left the room.

I stood there, staring at the ground, feeling confused and worried.

Greyson finally spoke up. "I don't know why you didn't leave with your friends."

"I want to know what happened to Nancy."

"I don't know what happened."

"I don't believe you."

"I don't care what you believe, Meg. You should have listened to your friend. What we had was about nothing more than sex."

"I don't care." I bit my lip as I lied. His words had cut me to the core. I'd really thought we were beyond that stage.

"If you're staying, you better get back outside. The tests will be starting soon."

"Okay." I nodded and glanced at him. He was surveying me with an odd light in his eyes.

He sighed. "You shouldn't have stayed, Meg."

"I couldn't leave," I whispered, and he nodded back at me.

"That's what I was afraid of."

***

I didn't go back outside right away. I couldn't face the others and the questions in their eyes. I needed to compose myself, and I wanted to check to see if Nancy was back in the room. Part of me knew that she wouldn't be there, but I was hoping beyond hope that she would have shown back up.

I quickly walked into our room and looked around. I stopped as I looked at my bed and the messy sheets. I was pretty confident that I had made my bed in the morning, like I always did. My breathing slowed as I looked around the room again to see if anything else looked askew. Nothing else seemed off, so I walked over to the bed and pulled off the duvet and the sheets to see if someone had left a note for me, but there was nothing there.

I threw the bedding back onto the bed and was about to walk back out of the room when I saw something shiny glittering underneath Nancy's bed. I ran back and quickly pulled it out, and I was surprised to see a diary. I opened it slowly, feeling bad for invading Nancy's privacy, but I needed to see what she had written in case there were any clues inside.

The diary appeared to have been started a long time ago, as the first entries were about some guy named Hunter who she appeared to have been in love with while in school. There was a lot of angst and emotion, and it seemed like Nancy had really had the bug for him. I flicked through the pages quickly, not wanting to read about her obviously unrequited and painful school crush. I flipped back a few pages, when I realized that my eyes had flickered over an entry about Maria.

"*Maria is bringing her new boyfriend home this weekend. Mom and Dad are excited that she's coming home, but that's because they don't know the truth. I can't believe that Maria is stripping now. I hope Ryan doesn't find out she's coming home. He's going to flip a switch. It's so unfair that Maria has two guys and I have none. I wish that Hunter would notice me ...*"

I stopped reading then, as it seemed that the writing changed pretty quickly back to her crush on Hunter. I sat on her bed and thought for a moment about what I had just read. I assumed that Maria's boyfriend was Brandon. But what did she mean about the stripping? Had Maria been a stripper? And if so, did that mean that the club really was a strip joint? But who was Ryan? And why had Nancy been worried that he would find out about her new boyfriend? I flipped through again, more carefully this time, to see what else I could find. I paused on the next page as I saw another entry.

"Maria's boyfriend Brandon is gorgeous. One of the most gorgeous men I've ever seen. He makes Hunter look like a little boy. Maria told me that he's the best sex she's ever had. I tried not to show her how uneasy she made me feel as she went into detail. I don't think she knows I'm still a virgin. I don't ..."

I sat up straight as something hit me. Nancy was eighteen. And supposedly, Maria had dated Brandon ten years ago, Nancy would have been eight when all of this had gone down. Why would she have been writing about a boy she had a crush on at eight? And the sex thing? It didn't make sense. There was no way that an eight-year-old had written this diary.

So that meant one of two things: this was someone else's diary or this was written at a later date. Either way, this diary had been left here for a purpose. This wasn't a case of Nancy accidentally leaving her diary in the room. Whoever had left the diary in the room wanted me to see it.

I wanted to feel like Nancy had left this for me to see, but I didn't understand why she would have written so much about her high school crush Hunter if she'd wanted to give me clues about Maria. Who cared how she'd felt about Hunter? That wasn't going to help me now. I closed my eyes and tried to think carefully. Maybe there were clues in what she had written about Hunter? Maybe the whole diary was a clue.

My eyes popped open as I heard a noise outside the door. I stood up slowly and walked to the spot behind the door. I held my breath as the door slowly opened with me behind it. I clutched the diary to me in fear. Who was about to walk through the door?

I felt and heard two footsteps, but whoever was there didn't bother coming all the way into the room and the door closed again within seconds. I stayed where I was for about another minute, trying to control my breathing.

I looked at the time and realized that I needed to get back outside if I wanted to continue on at the club. Part of me didn't really understand why Greyson was letting me stay. He had to know that I was going to continue to investigate while I was here. His secret was nearly out. He had to know that I would expose his sex trafficking to the world.

I didn't understand why he hadn't made me leave with Brandon and Katie. He probably wanted a few more nights with me before he got rid of me. I was angry at myself for how excited I felt about spending more nights with Greyson. It wasn't even about the sex, though that was mind-numbingly brilliant. It was about just being with him and getting to know him, snippet by snippet.

I walked out of the room and to the bathroom quickly. As I entered, I grabbed a plastic bag I saw on the ground and walked into one of the restrooms. I placed the diary into the plastic bag and tied it carefully and tightly, making sure that there were no small holes at the top of the bag. I opened the top of the toilet and peered inside; the water made me pause, but I knew there was nowhere else I could hide the diary. I dropped it in and moved the top back in place before slowly opening the door and walking out of the bathroom again.

"There you are, Meg." Patsy nodded at me as I walked back into the courtyard. "Decided to rejoin us?"

"Sorry, I, uh, wanted to check on Nancy."

"She's gone." Her eyes expressed concern as she spoke.

"I guess so."

"Is everyone ready for their tests today?" she continued, and I stood to the side.

I could see both David and Elizabeth trying to make eye contact with me. I looked around the group of girls and I realized that at least five of the girls were gone.

"Yes, Meg?" Patsy looked at me.

"Did some of the girls drop out? I see some are missing."

"No, they've been moved." Her eyes flashed at me.

"Can I ask where they've been moved to?"

"No." Her voice was harsh. "I wouldn't push it if I were you, Meg."

David gave me a look then. I could tell from his eyes that he was worried. I bit my lip as I stood there. David didn't know what had happened to Nancy. That meant that Nancy hadn't told him she was leaving or she hadn't left because she'd wanted to. I shivered even though it wasn't very cold.

I needed to go back and read more of the diary. I needed to know what else Nancy was trying to tell me. Or at least what someone else wanted me to think she was trying to tell me.

Patsy silently escorted me to my first room. I wanted to ask her if she knew what was really going on at the club, but I knew she wouldn't answer me. She was loyal to a fault.

"Are you coming in with me?" I turned towards Patsy as we arrived at the door.

"No." She stood there and pursed her lips. "I just wanted to make sure you made it here and didn't get lost."

"Excuse me?"

"I wouldn't make a habit of wandering around the club. You may find that you get lost, and you know what happens to people when they get lost once too often."

"No…"

"Sometimes they're never found." Her eyes pierced into mine and she opened the door. "I think you'll find that your test is about to start."

I walked into the room without answering her. Was she threatening me? Was there no one I could trust? I wished that

Katie had stayed behind with me. Though I wasn't sure how I could have asked her. If I'd told her everything I knew and suspected, she never would have let me stay.

The door closed behind me with a slam, and I sighed before looking around to see what my first task was going to be. I frowned as I observed the scene in front of me. This was a different kind of room. There was a long wooden table directly across from the door. On the table, there were about twenty different bottles of liquor with chasers. To the right of the table, I noticed some small packets. I swallowed hard as I walked closer to inspect the bags. My eyes widened as I realized that I was staring at bags of drugs. From what I could tell, I could see a bag of weed and a bag of cocaine, and there were pills in the other bags. I heard a thud and took a step back to look around. I could feel the warmth in my cheeks as I stood there. This wasn't what I had expected at all. Was Greyson a drug dealer? I stared at the table again, trying to figure out what my test was, as I couldn't see any pieces of paper. I stared at the table again to see if there was some sort of clue on the table, but if there was, I couldn't figure it out.

"Enjoy yourself," a smooth voice suddenly spoke into the room, and the lights dimmed.

I froze as I waited for Greyson to come into the room. I turned around and stared at the door, anticipating his entrance.

"Relax," the voice said again, and it was then that I noticed the glittering lights in the corner.

I walked over to see what was flashing and realized that it was a sound system. I pressed play and pulsing trance music blasted out of the speakers. I quickly turned it off and walked back to the table to see if there was anything I had missed.

I must have stood in the room doing nothing for about twenty minutes before the lights came back on and the voice said, "Testing done." I opened the door, feeling slightly disappointed that Greyson hadn't come to visit me. I'd been hoping that he would come and see me, that he would show me that he was thinking of me, despite what he had said.

I exited the room, but there was no Greyson and no Patsy waiting for me. I ran to the bathroom then so that I could read some more of Nancy's journal before my next testing. I let out a sigh of relief as I walked in and saw that the bathroom was empty. I entered the stall and pulled back the top of the toilet. Then I took the plastic bag out eagerly and quickly removed the diary, flicking through it until I reached the last entry I had read.

"I heard Maria crying last night. She was sobbing and I didn't know what to say to her. I've never seen her like that before. Not even when she broke up with Ryan. She was banging the walls hard with her fist. I was scared she was going to punch a hole in the walls. I went to her room to say something, but I saw her boyfriend in there with her. He was just staring at her, not doing anything. I know he saw me because he frowned as he made eye contact with me. I was scared when he looked at me. But then he turned away and walked over to Maria. All he kept saying was, 'I'm sorry,

but this was a mistake, I don't love you." That only made it worse. Maria grabbed a lamp and tried to hit him. I saw him get angry. I should have done something. I wish I'd done something now. If I had done something, maybe she wouldn't have died. But today she was all smiles to the parents. And so was he."

I stilled as I read the passage. Something was off, but I wasn't sure exactly what it was. I reread it again and tried to figure it out and then I realized it was the tense. I reread the sentence "If I had done something, maybe she wouldn't have died" again. From all accounts, Maria was still alive the day after Nancy had seen her crying. So if this had been a true entry or recounting from the past, that would never have been written. She wouldn't have known that Maria was going to die.

The passage confirmed my earlier thoughts. These entries had been written recently, and I was almost positive that they'd been written by Nancy. That meant she had written and left this for me deliberately. It also made me think that there was a possibility that she hadn't disappeared when I thought she had disappeared. What if she had left this in the room when I was in Greyson's office with Brandon and Katie? But why would she have just disappeared and not told me or David? I sighed and opened the diary again.

"Brandon Hastings is Maria's boyfriend's name. He's not a good man. He is evil. Yes, I said it. He broke Maria until there was nothing left.

But she always chose bad men. Really bad men. I don't want anyone else to get hurt. I'm scared he's going to kill someone for revenge. He doesn't know everything. He doesn't understand. He hates the big boss. The real club owner. There was really only ever one. He wants to hurt him. He knows his weakness. I'm scared that this time it's going to be bloody. He's not right in the head. He's not the man you think he is. He'll murder. Maria loved Brandon, but Greyson held her heart. That's why he's really mad."

I dropped the diary on the ground and sat back. My head was pounding. I grabbed the diary up again and read the last sentence again. Had Maria dated Greyson as well? Was that why Brandon and Greyson's friendship had disintegrated? Was that why Greyson accepted responsibility for everything that had gone down? Was Greyson the one who'd caused Maria's death?

I reread the entry again and my brain started throbbing. I wasn't really sure what Nancy was trying to tell me. The more I read it, the more it seemed that Brandon was the bad one. It was oddly written, and I couldn't tell if she was trying to tell me if Brandon or Greyson was the angry one. The more I read it, the more I was convinced that it was actually Brandon who was the evil one.

As I sat there, I remembered how Brandon had treated Katie back in college when he'd found out she was eighteen. He'd been a horrible person and done a really horrible thing. He'd treated her like shit, and even though I knew he'd had a reason to be upset, I felt that what he'd done had been unacceptable.

I flipped the page to continue reading. I had about five more minutes before I had to rush to my next test. As I turned the page, I realized that this was the last entry in the journal.

"Hunter is older than me. Has more secrets. Doesn't believe in love. I'm a fool like my sister. But what wouldn't one do for love? Swimming is good for the body. The truth lies in the water. Trust in what you feel. That's what I say. Don't venture into the deep end. It's easy to drown."

And that was it. I was even more confused than before. What was she talking about? Why was she mentioning Hunter again? Was Hunter the code name for someone at the club? My heart stopped for a second as the thought hit me. *Is Hunter really Greyson?* Was Nancy dating Greyson? His description sounded just like Greyson to me.

I stilled as I heard two girls walk into the bathroom.

"God, if I get another stupid test, I'm going to scream."

"Mine was pretty cool," her friend said. "I got to smoke some pretty dope weed."

"What?" The other girl sounded jealous.

"Yeah, there was some coke as well. But I didn't see it until the end."

"Did you take it?"

"Nah." The girl paused. "Well, just a little bit."

"Let me have some."

"Not now. We can do some tonight."

"That's what I'm talking about." The other girl sounded excited. "Let's get fucking high."

"Fuck yeah. I was starting to think this place was a dump, but now I know they got the goods for free."

"Better than selling your body, eh?"

"Shit. I was with a guy who used to give me molly for a blowjob." The girl sounded nonchalant. "It was worth it."

"I'd love to give Greyson a blowjob Or even fucking David. He's hot."

"I heard Elizabeth was fucking Frank. I'd do him."

"He's not hot."

"He's all right." The girl laughed. "Okay, don't hate me. But I fucked David last night."

"You bitch! You did not!"

"Well, he came to my room and—"

I sat there still as a stone waiting to hear more, but someone else walked into the room.

"You okay, girls?" Patsy's voice vibrated in the room.

"Yes," one of the girls said. This time her voice was not as loud or excited.

"Then I suggest you go back to the test rooms."

"Yes, ma'am."

"Also, please give me the package in your pocket."

"What?"

"I know you took something from the room. Please hand it to me." Patsy's voice was firm.

"I don't know what you're talking about."

"The package."

"Here you go." The girl huffed. "I didn't even know what it was."

"Get to your next test rooms, please."

I sat in the stall and waited until I was pretty confident that they had all left. I exited slowly after storing the diary back in the top of the toilet. I walked to my next test room quickly. My mind was spinning again. I felt like every time I thought I had a new lead, something else cropped up to make me doubt what I thought I knew.

I walked into my next room with my thoughts in a whirl. I didn't even look to see what the new room contained since I was so caught up in the hurricane that was swirling around in me.

"Hi, Meg." His voice was soft and unexpected.

"Greyson." I looked up at him in surprise, not able to stop the acceleration of my heart. "What are you doing here?"

"I figured you missed me or something."

"I saw you this morning." I knew my words sounded shaky.

"Maybe I missed you." He shrugged as he eyes sought out mine.

"Yeah, right." I rolled my eyes. "What do you really want?"

"A kiss." He walked toward me with the confidence of a man who knew he could have any woman he wanted.

I stared at his face clinically, trying to understand why this man made me lose my mind. It wasn't like I hadn't seen handsome men before. Granted, I'd never dated or made love to a man whose blue eyes had sent shivers down my spine like his did. I'd never seen a man whose jaw had quite that angle and whose golden locks felt soft and silky to the touch. I'd never been touched by a man whose fingers were rough and gentle at the same time. I'd never tasted a man whose very essence reminded me of manna from heaven.

"That's it?" I swallowed as he stopped in front of me

"Unless you want more?" His eyes sparkled at me, and I could see a question in them that had nothing to do with him kissing me.

"What if I want less?"

"It'd be hard to want less than I have to give." The smile left his face, but he continued to gaze impenetrably into my eyes.

"You'd be surprised."

"Why didn't you leave with Katie and Brandon?"

"Why did you let me stay?"

"You shouldn't be here, you know."

"Why?"

"You'll be the undoing of me." He grimaced.

"Scared you'll go to jail?"

"No."

"Really? I would be if I were you."

"I'm not scared of jail." He shrugged. "There are worse demons in my mind."

"Oh." I frowned. "What made you the man you are, Greyson?"

"My dad kept a woman in the basement."

"What?" I whispered and looked up at him in shock. "Are you joking?"

He continued talking as if he hadn't heard me. "She was like his sex slave. He would go down every night and do things with her. I didn't know at first. I thought he was grieving, like I was. But one night, I heard noises, so I went to investigate and I saw him fucking her."

"Oh my."

"She lived in the basement." His eyes looked at me and he cocked his head. "But she wasn't locked there. She was free to leave. But she stayed there. Living for the night, when my dad would go down and fuck her."

"Why didn't he let her come up into the house and live?"

"He didn't care about her," he spat out. "He loved my mom. He would never sully her name. But he had needs. All men have needs, Meg. Needs have nothing to do with love."

"So what happened?" I asked softly, feeling my heart breaking at his words.

"You're so beautiful." His finger caressed my cheek. "When I look into your eyes, I find myself getting lost in your beauty."

"Thank you," I whispered, not knowing how to respond.

"Don't thank me. It's not a compliment." His finger slid down to my lips and he pushed his finger into my mouth. I lightly sucked it, and we just stared at each other. "I could get you to do whatever I want, couldn't I?"

"No." I shook my head and bit down on his finger hard. "You can't control me."

"Feisty." He laughed and pulled his finger out. He changed the subject again and turned around. "Do you think men run the world, Meg?"

"Yes, but not because they are better than women. They just have less compassion. They dictate and take what they want without any real care as to how their actions affect others."

He turned around and looked at me then, a small smile on his face. "But women, they have this compassion, yes?"

"Most of us do."

"Can a woman forgive the devil?"

"It's not for a woman to forgive the devil. It's for the devil to forgive the devil."

"What does it matter if he forgives himself?"

"For the devil to forgive himself, he has to acknowledge he's done wrong. That's the biggest step." I reached over and touched his cheek. "Once he realizes he's done wrong, he can seek redemption."

"Why do you do this to me?" He pulled me towards him and stared down at me for a second before his lips came crushing down on mine.

I melted against him and closed my eyes as we kissed. I breathed in all of him as his tongue invaded my mouth. His fingers reached into my hair and pulled roughly. I squirmed against him as he pulled me closer to him. I opened my eyes as he bit down on my lower lip.

"Good. I like to see the emotions in your eyes as I kiss you," he growled and then continued his exploration of my mouth.

I kissed him back fervently, sucking on his tongue eagerly. He was my drug, and I couldn't get enough of him. I felt his hands fall to my butt, and I ran my hands to his back and let my fingers run up and down urgently. I eagerly slipped my fingers under his shirt and scraped my fingernails against his skin. I felt his sharp intake of breath as he felt my fingers grazing his skin.

"I can do rough as well, you know." His fingers squeezed my ass tighter, and I gasped as he pushed me back against the wall. My neck fell back and his lips closed down on the large expanse of skin that was showing. I felt his teeth biting me hard and then he used his tongue, gently soothing the area.

"Greyson," I groaned against him.

"Yes?" He paused and looked at me.

"Nothing." I closed my eyes again. I didn't want to speak. I just wanted to feel. His actions matched my feelings about this situation. It was painful and sweet. I sighed as he slowly pulled away from me.

"You should do your test."

"I don't even know what it is." I smiled ruefully and he grinned back at me.

"I guess I didn't give you time."

"No, you didn't."

"Okay, check." He took another step back, and I looked around the room curiously. The room was larger than most of the other rooms. It looked like some sort of playroom. There was a pool table and a poker table. There was a TV in the corner with a game system connected.

"I have no idea what I'm supposed to do in here." I looked up at him. "Who comes up with these tests? They're so random."

"Nothing in life is random." Greyson looked at me contemplatively. "Come." He grabbed my hand and pulled me to a corner of the room that had an armoire. "Open it up."

"Okay …?" I looked at him questioningly for a second before opening it up. The armoire was filled with bikinis, and I looked at him curiously. "What are these for? Strip poker?"

"What are most bikinis for?"

I shrugged. "The beach?"

"No." Greyson walked to the other side of the room, and I saw a dartboard on the wall.

"What are you doing?" I called out to him, but he ignored me. Instead, I watched as he opened a cleverly concealed door. "What's in there?"

"Come and see." He smiled at me, and I walked over to him quickly. I stared through the door and gasped. There was a huge Olympic-size pool in the room. Next to the pool, I could see a hot tub, and there were rose petals on the ground.

"What's this?"

"A pool."

"I see that, but why?"

"Want to go swimming?"

"I don't have a swim …" I started and then stopped. "I guess that's why the bikinis are there."

"Shall we swim?"

"I don't want to wear a bikini that someone else has worn."

"You don't have to." He grinned as he pulled off his shirt and threw it on the ground.

I stared at his naked chest and swallowed hard. *Shit, he was hot.* There was a light spattering of hair on his pecs, and I ran my fingers through it. It felt so soft. I ran my fingers across it again and then I lightly squeezed his nipples. Greyson stilled as I touched him, and I looked up to see a small smile on his face.

"About that swim …" He chuckled and nodded towards the pool.

"I don't want to wear a used bikini."

"As I said before, you don't have to."

"Do you have a new one for me?"

"No." He winked at me, and I watched as he took his shoes off, discarded his socks, and then unzipped his pants.

I swallowed hard as he pulled his pants and briefs off in one swoop. His cock stood to attention and he stretched in front of me. His muscles rippled and I stared at his body, barely able to think about anything other than how sexy he was. I watched as he walked away from me and then dived into the pool and started doing laps. I stared at his clothes on the ground and laughed.

"Meg, you're so slow," I whispered to myself as I realized what he had been saying. There was no bikini for me to wear. He wanted me to go skinny-dipping with him. I walked into the room and watched as he swam.

"Are you coming in?"

"No." I shook my head as I stood at the side of the pool.

"That's a shame." He started swimming again and I watched his body make its way through the water. He swam gracefully, barely making a ripple.

I stood there, unsure about what I should do. I really wanted to pull my clothes off and join him, but all I could think about was Nancy's journal entry about the pool. I bit my lip as I stared at Greyson while he swam. I wanted to join him, but a part of me was scared.

Then I heard a noise and I turned to look in the test room quickly. My body froze as I caught a glimpse of a body moving in the room. I walked back to the room as quietly as I could, but it was empty.

"What's wrong?" Greyson's voice made me jump as I realized that he had gotten out of the pool and was now behind me.

"Nothing." I shook my head and gasped as he pulled me back toward his naked, wet body.

"Join me in the pool, Meg," he whispered in my ear urgently as I felt his hands reach up to my breasts. "Please." His hard cock pushed against my butt and I swallowed as his breath teased my ear.

I stood there with my back to him and closed my eyes. What was going on here? If I didn't find out soon, I knew I was going to go crazy.

CHAPTER FOUR

Greyson

20 Years Ago

"I got the keys." I dangled them in front of Brandon's face. "We're doing this, bitch."

"Your dad gave you the money?" Brandon looked surprised but excited.

"I threatened to tell everyone about the women he keeps." I shrugged. "He doesn't want people to know he's not the grieving widower."

"He's got more than one now?"

"One in the basement. One in an apartment in Harlem."

"Oh."

"Who cares? We'll just call it a graduation gift."

"Yeah. How much did he give you?"

"Ten million."

"He really didn't want that news out, huh?"

"What are you talking about? He's just proud that his only son graduated *magna cum laude* from Harvard." I stared at him. "And it didn't hurt that I had photos of his dungeon— whips and all."

Brandon's eyes widened. "Shit."

"More like fuck yeah. We can have a dungeon at the club."

"What do we need a dungeon for?"

"Kinky sex. Do I have to spell it out?"

"I don't know." Brandon frowned.

"You don't have to partake."

"Well, I'm not saying no." He laughed.

"Fucker." I walked into the kitchen of the apartment we shared. "Want a beer?"

"Nah," he called back. "So when can I see the building?"

"We can go now if you want." I grinned excitedly, adrenaline pumping through my veins. I was excited to see that my vision was finally coming true.

"Yeah. Let's go."

"Be warned, it's not fixed up yet."

"Oh shit, it's a hell hole?"

"It's epic, dude. It's huge. It's perfect. It just needs some TLC."

"You mean money?" Brandon rolled his eyes.

"That would help."

"I guess I need to contribute."

"That would help." I grinned.

"You know my dad expects me to work at his company."

"That's fine. I'll run the day-to-day at the club."

"I can get my hands on five million pretty easily." Brandon looked at me questioningly. "That enough?"

"That'll do to start." I nodded. "Let's go. We can take a cab."

"Shit. I can't believe we're doing this."

"I've got some girls coming tomorrow."

"For what?"

"To get the party started." I grinned.

"You're bad," he laughed.

"Hey, bad is better than fucked up. Which is what most women call me." I chuckled, feeling high on life.

"They don't even know what fucked up is." Brandon rolled his eyes as we made our way to the street corner. "You don't promise them shit."

"Exactly. That's why I don't feel bad. What you see is what you get."

"No promises and no lies."

"Exactly. It's not my fault if some dumbass girl wants to fool herself into thinking it's about anything more than sex."

"That's why we run the world. We think with our brains and fuck with our heads." Brandon laughed and I groaned.

"Is the protégé trying to outdo his master with these comments?" I laughed and stared at my friend as we got into the cab.

"Wait until the girls start at the club before you ask anyone to call you master." Brandon punched me in the shoulder. "Or I'll have to take you out."

"You'll take me out?" I raised an eyebrow at him and flexed my biceps. "Don't let my handsome good looks fool you, bro."

"Shut up. What's going on tomorrow with the girls? You need some help?"

"Thought your dad wanted you to start tomorrow?"

"I can always make time for hotties."

"That's my job done, folks. I've corrupted him." I chuckled and sat back in the cab.

I tried to ignore the guilt in my heart. I wasn't really proud that I had dragged my best friend to the dark side with me. A part of me wished that he had been able to take me to his side back when we were in high school. But it seemed that evil always won out. Back in the day, it had been me and him arguing over how to treat women, and now there was no arguing. We were both dogs.

***

"How did the interviews go?" Brandon turned up in his suit, looking very much like a young businessman.

"Eh, nothing special." I shrugged. "None of the girls were acceptable."

"I met some guys in the office. Some guys from Yale and Brown. They're looking for a new place to relax in the evenings. I told them I might know of a place."

"Oh yeah?" I sat back. "What did they say?"

"'How much?'" Brandon laughed. "We haven't spoken about the fees yet."

"I'm thinking $100,000 a year," I said straight-faced.

Brandon shook his head. "There's clubs in Miami that charge $100,000."

"$250,000 then."

"That's better." Brandon smiled.

"Then we need high-quality girls."

"We need high-quality everything." He nodded. "How much do we have left?"

"About two and half million," I sighed. "The structural issues were worse than I thought."

"I can get more. What about you?"

I shook my head. "My trust fund doesn't pay out for three more years."

"How much more do you think we need?"

"Another ten million."

"I'll do a transfer tomorrow."

"You sure?"

"I'm sure. What are friends for?"

"That's why I chose you as my partner." I grinned and he laughed.

"Uh huh."

"I can't believe we're doing this." I looked at him. "We're really doing this, Brandon."

"I never had any doubt."

"Really?"

"Anything you put your mind to, you do."

"Thanks."

"It's not a compliment." Brandon looked at me with a sad face. "Are we doing the right thing?"

"What do you mean?"

"I don't know. It's exciting, but I can't explain it. It just seems off. Like we're doing something bad."

"We're providing a service."

"I know, but who are these women?"

"We're not providing escorts." I frowned. "Or prostitutes."

"But we're not saying no to sex."

"They're adults. They can do what they want."

"What about the dungeons and the rooms?"

"What about them?"

"What if someone gets hurt?"

"We won't let anyone get hurt."

"If you're sure." Brandon didn't look convinced. "I don't want to—"

"Look, Brandon, these women want it just as badly as we do. They might lie and say it's about love, but it's not. It's about them getting fucked hard and good. It's about them getting money. It's about them thinking they're getting something. They don't give two shits."

"I don't know." Brandon frowned. "What about love?"

"Love?" I laughed. "What's love? Some emotion that twists your head and your heart? What is this, Brandon? You're not going all Ward Cleaver on me, are you? You're not telling me you want two point four children and a fucking house on Long Island?"

"That's not what I'm saying. I'm just saying that—"

A soft voice interrupted. "Hi, excuse me." I looked up. A sweet, demure-looking girl stepped into the room. "Sorry, I'm here for the interview. I'm not late, am I?"

"No, not late at all." I smiled at her and winked at Brandon. Now, this was what I was talking about. She was fresh-faced and sweet, with the right amount of sex appeal.

"Great." She looked back and forth between me and Brandon. "I had trouble finding the place."

"No worries. We're new."

"I know." She nodded.

"Okay, so what experience do you have?"

"Depends on what the job is." She grinned at me and I laughed.

"The job depends on your skills."

"I've got plenty of skills. Typing, dictation, dancing ..." She did a pirouette and grinned again.

"What about lap dancing?" Brandon spoke up and I frowned.

"Brandon, have some class." I shook my head at him and then looked back at the girl. "Sorry about that. My business partner is new to this."

"No worries." She smiled at me and leaned forward. "But if you want to know, I can give one heck of a lap dance."

"Oh yeah?" I sat back and grinned. "That doesn't hurt."

"Yeah, I'm pretty flexible." She ran her hands through her hair. "Or so I've been told."

"You can show me if you want." Brandon sat down on one of the chairs. "Show me what you're working with."

"Brandon, no. Just no." I shook my head at him again. "Sorry about that." I smiled at the girl sweetly, hoping she didn't realize that I was the real wolf in the room.

"Don't worry about it." She winked at me.

"You're hired." I leaned forward and shook her head. "Welcome to the private club."

***

"I can't believe I'm doing this." She looked behind at me as I fucked her from behind.

"Don't feel bad. Many women can't resist me."

"I never have sex on the first date, though." She giggled and then screamed as I increased my pace and squeezed her breasts.

"This isn't a date," I grunted as I slid in and out of her.

"Oh, but—"

"Shut up for a second, please." I grabbed her hips and held her back as I increased my pace again. "Fuck yeah, I'm about to come." I closed my eyes as I felt my load about to blow.

"Me too," she moaned, and I felt her start to twist her hips on my cock.

"Oh yeah," I groaned. The movement of her hips did it and I felt myself coming. I pulled out of her quickly, peeled the cum-filled condom off, and jumped up.

"Oh." She looked up at me with a disappointed glance. I knew she hadn't orgasmed, but I didn't care. She was no one to me. And she was a fool if she thought this meant anything. I'd only known her for an hour. Just because I'd hired her didn't mean anything.

"You can take care of it if you want." I shrugged as I zipped my pants up. "Brandon won't be back for another fifteen minutes."

"What?" She looked up at me in confusion.

"Use your fingers." I looked down at her and tried not to roll my eyes at her stupidity. "Get yourself off."

"Oh, I can't …" She blushed.

"Think of it as an audition." I grinned. "Some of our patrons may ask you to do this. Let's see if you can." I stood there looking down at her, waiting to see what she was going to do.

"Okay." She nodded, lay flat on her back, and closed her eyes. I watched as her fingers worked their way between her legs and she started rubbing her clit. She moaned, and I knew the exact moment that she got into it. Her legs were trembling and her fingers started moving quickly.

"That's it, Patsy," I spoke softly. "Make yourself come." I watched as she rolled around the floor for a few more seconds before I took out my phone and left the room so I could go to check my messages.

CHAPTER FIVE

Meg

Present Day

"I think I saw someone in the room," I whispered back to Greyson as he ground his cock against me. The water from his wet body was soaking into my clothes and I was starting to feel sticky.

"Are you sure?" He nibbled on my ear.

"Yes." I nodded. "I'm pretty sure there was someone in the room."

"Maybe it was one of the cleaning ladies?" He pulled me around to face him. His eyes grew concerned as he took in my face. "Are you okay, Meg?"

"It just gave me a fright. Seeing someone in there."

"No one will do anything to you. I'm here."

"Yeah." I looked up at him and smiled weakly. "I guess you're going to take care of me."

"Of course." He leaned down and kissed my nose. "As soon as you take care of me."

"All you think about is sex."

"I wasn't talking about sex." He pulled back from me then and his expression changed. "Do you want to swim?"

"Why not." I stood on tiptoes and kissed him. "Why the hell not!"

"You always surprise me, Meg."

"Why's that?"

"You're different," he said and then groaned. "And I couldn't have used a more cliché expression."

"How am I different?"

"You didn't jump into the pool as soon as you saw me take off my clothes."

"Are you really that vain?" I laughed.

"Yes." He grinned back at me and then grabbed my hand. "And yes, I'm really hard right now as well." I felt my hand against his hardness and I squeezed instinctively. He groaned as my fingers rubbed off the drops of water. "Oh, Meg."

"Why do you always make me touch your ..." I paused.

"My what?"

"You know?"

"No." He chucked. "My nose?"

"Yeah, you always make me touch your nose." I rolled my eyes.

"Ask a silly question, be told a silly answer."

"Are you calling me silly?" I giggled.

"Would I do such a thing?"

"Yes."

"Let's go swim."

"I'll race you." I pulled away from him and ran to the pool. I pulled off items of clothing as I ran—well mainly my top. I tried to pull the rest off, but it was too hard to do as I was running. I groaned inside at my major fail at seductive disrobing.

Greyson caught up with me at the side of the pool and laughed. "What was that?"

I tried not to stare at his body as he was making my heart palpitate. He was too sexy for his own good. It was like Michelangelo had carved his body out of stone. It was so perfect. I couldn't resist myself and reached over and ran my fingers down his washboard abs and shivered. Greyson stared at me and gave me a small smile.

"No one's touched me so reverently before."

"I don't know why not." I smiled back at him weakly. "You're perfect."

"We both know that's not true."

"Well, your body is pretty darn perfect."

"I wish I were perfect in other ways." He looked at me wistfully. "I've never wished for a different life before now. My philosophy is life gives us what we can take and we have to make the best of it. But somehow with you, I wish it had been different. Maybe if my life had been different from the beginning, I'd be a different man now. A better man."

"Why do you wish you were a better man?" I asked with my heart in my throat.

"Probably for the same reason you wish I were a better man," he answered astutely.

"I don't even know you." I shrugged and stared at the pool. The water was such a calming and beautiful blue. The serenity of the setting belied the churning of the hurricane in my heart and stomach.

"I guess sometimes you don't have to know someone very long to know you like them."

"Or dislike them," I quipped back.

"I wonder how things would have been different if we'd met in a different setting," he continued.

"What sort of setting?" I looked up at him, wondering what he was thinking and feeling inside.

"Like a grocery store." He laughed. "If we'd bumped into each other at Whole Foods, or maybe even Trader Joe's. You'd be buying a French baguette and some brie. I'd be buying a nice bottle of Pinot Grigio or maybe even a cabernet."

"And then what?" I asked breathlessly as he stopped.

"You have to take off another piece of clothing before I continue." He nodded at me and I rolled my eyes, but I still removed my pants and shoes. He watched me with narrowed eyes then, surveying my nearly naked body with eager lust. "Beautiful," he muttered as he looked back into my eyes. "I'd look at you as you bumped into me and I'd wonder—"

"Who said it was me bumping into you?" I interrupted.

"I'm not clumsy."

"Neither am I."

"Like I was saying … As you bumped into me"—he grinned at me then—"I would see how beautiful and witty you were and I'd think to myself, 'Maybe we could pair our wine and bread together.'"

"That's what you would say?" I laughed, feeling young and happy at our banter. "You'd say, 'Let's pair our wine and bread together'? To a girl you just bumped into at the grocery store?"

"No, that's not what I'd say." He cocked his head and stared at me with a sly smile. "If you want to know what I'd say, please take off another item of clothing."

"Fine." I rolled my eyes, but inside I was shivering with excitement. I looked down at my body in consideration for a moment and then took off my bra. Greyson's eyes dilated as he stared at my naked breasts, and his fingers reached over to cup them gently. He took a step towards me and I moaned as I felt his hardness brush against my legs.

"I would say, 'You have beautiful eyes.'" He looked down at me as his fingers gently rubbed my nipples. "I would say that I had a bottle of wine, but no bread and cheese. I'd give you a sweet smile." He looked at me. "Much like this. And I'd ask if you'd like to go on a picnic."

"A picnic?" I asked and then gasped as his fingers pinched my nipples.

"Of course. A cutesy picnic in Central Park."

"I can't see you on a picnic in Central Park," I laughed, and he smiled back at me.

"Well, this is if I had had a different life. If I'd had a different life, I'd love picnics in Central Park."

"I see." I hoped he would continue with his story.

"So then I'd wait for your answer. I'd hope your answer would be yes. Then maybe I'd buy some chocolate-covered strawberries as well, but I'd hide them until later on the date." His eyes glittered at me. "I wouldn't want you thinking I had any ideas."

I laughed. "But of course you'd have ideas."

"Well, of course I would. That much of me wouldn't be different." He chuckled, and as I stared at him, I realized how young he looked in that moment. How carefree. My heart stilled as I realized that this was the Greyson I wish existed.

"And then what?" I prodded him, needing him to continue.

"And then ..." He pulled me closer towards him. "And then we'd go to the park. I think I'd take you to Midtown and we'd go in around West 50th."

"There's an entrance there?"

"There's an entrance near there, I'm sure." He shrugged. "And we'd sit on the green grass and laugh. I'd tell you some jokes and show you some magic tricks."

"How old are we in this dream?" I raised an eyebrow at him, and he smacked my bottom. "Ow."

"Listen." He pulled me closer to him. "Then we'd lie back and stare at the sky and the birds."

"Hopefully it's not a grey day," I mumbled, and he smacked my butt again. I yelped at the touch of his hand against me, but he only smiled.

"At some point, you'd realize that I was utterly attractive and desirable and you'd reach over and kiss me."

"Actually, I think I'd be waiting on you to kiss me."

"Well, I think you wouldn't be able to resist me and you'd reach over and kiss me lightly." He leaned down. "And then you'd kiss me like this." His lips touched mine and he pressed them down lightly and gave me a sweet kiss before pulling back. "And I'd be sitting there thinking, 'Wow. What happened?'"

"Uh huh," I whispered breathlessly.

"And I'd be hoping you'd do it again."

"Yes." I looked up at him, wanting to feel the softness of his lips on mine again.

"Yes, you would?" He stared into my eyes, searching for an answer, and I nodded.

"Yes, I would do it again. All over again."

His lips crushed down on mine again, but this time they moved with deliberate speed, as if they were on a mission. His tongue entered my mouth, and I reached up and grasped the ends of his hair. His chest hair teased my breasts and his fingers massaged my back as we kissed. I felt his cock pressed up against my stomach and I pushed myself against him harder. Our bodies were both slightly cold, so I pushed into him harder so that we could build up our body heat.

His fingers fell to my ass, and he pulled me closer to him while he squeezed my butt. I moaned as his lips left mine and he kissed down my neck to my breasts. His tongue gently licked my nipples before his lips clamped down and sucked on them. I closed my eyes as I felt the warmth of his mouth consuming me.

His fingers started playing with my other nipple, and I gripped his shoulders as I felt my legs starting to weaken with desire.

Greyson pulled away from me and then kissed down my stomach. His teeth grabbed the front of my panties and he gently tugged them down. When they reached my ankles, I quickly stepped out of them and Greyson growled in satisfaction. He stood back up slowly and grinned at me before diving into the pool. I watched as he swam underwater and then popped up on the other side of the pool.

"Come and join me, Meg."

I dived into the pool before I could talk myself out of it. The cold water shocked my skin as I swam, and I stayed underwater, trying to get my body to adjust the cool temperature faster. I swam quickly and did a quick turn when I reached the other side and did another lap. After about thirty seconds, my body adjusted to the temperature, and I lay back in the water and floated on my back.

"I didn't know you were such a mermaid." Greyson swam up to me, and I started to tread water so that I could look at him instead of the ceiling.

"Well, they don't call me Ariel for nothing." I grinned at him and he splashed me. "Hey!" I splashed him back and he laughed.

"You're going to get my hair wet!" he screamed and I laughed.

"I'm sorry to tell you this, but it's wet already."

"So are you." He licked his lips.

"Yes, I am wet." I rolled my eyes. "I am in the water."

"That's not the kind of wet I'm talking about." He swam closer to me, and I felt his fingers reaching in between my legs. As they caressed my clit, I found my feet kicking faster in the pool.

"You're a bad boy."

"You wouldn't want it any other way."

"I thought you were trying to be good now."

"No." He shook his head and stared at me. "I said if life had been different, I might have been a different person. I might have been good. But life wasn't different and I'm still me, and I'm as bad as they come."

"You're not really bad."

"Oh, really?" He grinned at me, and I felt him pull my legs around his waist. "You don't think I'm bad?"

"No." I gasped as I felt him enter me slowly.

"Not even now?" He laughed and pushed me back against the wall.

"No." I shook my head slowly and moaned as he increased the pace of his thrusts.

"Hold on to my back," he ordered as his hands gripped the side of the pool. I closed my eyes and gripped his slippery back. "Now lean back into the wall so that your body is floating up a little bit," he commanded, and I leaned back slightly, holding on to him tightly. "Don't worry, Meg. I'm not going to let go."

I kept my eyes closed as he spoke and concentrated on the pleasure filling my body and not his words. I knew that part of me wished that he truly meant his words. I wanted him to tell me that he was never going to let me go ever. But I dismissed the thoughts. I didn't want to become that girl. I didn't want to make this more than it was. Not to me and not to him. We barely knew each other.

Instead, I concentrated on the way his cock was moving inside of me so delicately and deliciously. It was a different experience, being in the pool and having sex. It felt different. Not necessarily more intense, but more unique. I could feel the water caressing me and I could hear the sound of the splashing as he took me. My breasts bobbled up and down in the water, gently grazing his chest, and my ass felt like it was floating in the water. It almost felt like I was weightless as we clung to each other.

"I think I'm going to come," he groaned into my ear and I opened my eyes to see his face. His eyes were full of desire, and he increased his pace. The water was splashing higher now, and I wrapped my legs around him tighter, enjoying watching him about to orgasm. "Are you nearly there?" he whispered and stilled, looking at me searchingly.

"No." I bit my lip as I spoke honestly and moved my hips against him gently.

"Oh, shit," he groaned, and I felt his body shuddering as he came inside of me. "Oh, Meg." He held on to me tight as his lips sought mine. He withdrew from me slowly and looked back up at me with a determined look in his eyes. "You didn't come?"

"No." I shook my head and he smiled wickedly.

"I guess I'll have to change that to a yes." He grabbed my body and held me as he swam to the steps. He pulled me out of the pool with him and quickly ran to get some towels. He came back with three large white towels and laid one flat on the side of the pool. "Lie down." He grabbed my hand and pulled me down to the towel. "Are you cold?" he asked as he noticed my shivering.

"I'm fine."

"Let me warm you up a bit." He grabbed another one of the towels, unfolded it, and gently started rubbing my body dry. "I don't want you to get a cold. How does this feel?"

"It feels nice." I nodded and smiled at him. It felt nice to be rubbed down by Greyson. It made me feel like he actually cared about me.

"Now, lie back and spread your legs." He grinned at me wickedly. "I've got some work to do."

I stared up at him and tried not to sigh. Just when I thought it might have been about more than sex, he said or did something that brought me back down to earth.

"You are so beautiful to me." Greyson stared at me and started singing.

"Is that a song?"

"No, it's a fact." He winked and then I felt his fingers kneading my breasts as he kissed my stomach and licked my belly button. "You look like an angel and you taste like a sinner."

"I don't feel like much of an angel," I groaned as he kissed farther down and buried his face in my pussy. "Oh, Greyson." I reached down and grabbed his hair. His tongue felt warm and soft against my coldness, and I squirmed beneath him as his lips sucked and kissed me. His tongue slowly moved back and forth on my clit, and I grabbed his hair harder. "Please," I moaned, wriggling around in ecstasy. I wanted to feel more of him everywhere. I needed to feel him inside of me.

Greyson didn't play games with me this time. His tongue entered me skillfully, teasing and tormenting me as his fingers played with my clit. I couldn't believe how exquisite the pleasure was. I could feel every nerve ending in my body tingling and crying out. I felt as if I were on the edge of a cliff and there was a cool breeze that was aching to push me over. I was so close to just falling and letting nature do what she wanted to with me. I was so close to becoming one with the wind. I just needed one last push.

I screamed out when Greyson pulled his tongue out of me. "No, don't stop!" I begged, not caring that I was squirming beneath him. My hands reached down and pushed his head back between my legs. "I'm so close," I whispered pitifully.

"Tell me how it feels," he growled at me and licked my clit again.

"It feels like I'm going to explode," I moaned. "Please."

"Please, who?"

"Greyson!" I cried out. He grinned and then pulled me up quickly.

"Get on all fours," he commanded me. "That's it."

I knelt on the ground and waited for what was next. Greyson swiveled me around so that my ass was facing him and I felt his thumb rubbing me gently.

"What are you doing?" I gasped and jumped slightly as he grazed my asshole.

"Don't worry, Meg." He laughed as he came up behind me. I felt the tip of his cock at my entrance, but instead of entering me, he gently rubbed my clit. I buckled forward slightly and he laughed again. "You're still so wet for me." I didn't answer him. Instead, I braced myself for the pleasure I knew was coming.

I didn't have to wait long. My first orgasm occurred as soon as he entered me. I felt my pussy walls tighten on his hard cock and my whole body shook as the orgasm hit me. That seemed to turn him on even more because he grabbed my hips and grunted as he moved in and out of me.

"I love to feel it when you orgasm." He groaned. "It makes me harder knowing that I'm responsible for bringing you so much pleasure."

"Oh, please don't stop." I gyrated my hips back into him, relishing in the fact that I could feel another orgasm building up.

"I'm sorry I didn't make you come in the pool." He sounded annoyed with himself. "I don't want you to think that I don't care about you being taken care of."

"It's okay." I moaned as I gripped the towel to steady myself. "You're making up for it now."

Greyson pulled out of me suddenly and flipped me onto my back before entering me again.

"I like looking into your eyes when I orgasm." He kissed me urgently as his cock filled me to the brim. "It makes it feel more special."

I looked into his eyes at that moment and there was a light there that I had never seen before. I felt my body burning in that moment. I felt so high and powerful. Everything felt heightened, and as we stared at each other, I felt like I was flying. My heart and my soul were soaring, and as we climaxed together, I knew that this was another moment that I wouldn't forget for the rest of my life.

***

I dried my skin with the large white fluffy towel Greyson had given me and tried not to let my feelings of guilt overwhelm me. I knew as sure as I knew that the sky was blue that I was falling for Greyson. Had already fallen for Greyson, if I were honest.

I wanted to laugh at the irony of it all. I was the girl who didn't believe in love at first sight. I was the girl who'd scoffed when friends told me they'd found 'the one' after a few dates. What was 'the one,' really? Was there really one person for everyone? I'd always thought that God had forgotten me. Where was my one? I'd somehow made it through life without any great loves and I didn't want Greyson to be the one.

My breath caught and I felt tears welling in my eyes as I realized the truth that I hadn't wanted to acknowledge. I was falling in love with Greyson Twining and I didn't want to. I didn't want my heart to skip every time I saw him. I didn't want my stomach to flip when I thought about him. I didn't want to be able to close my eyes and picture him next to me. I didn't want to be able to smell him in the air. I didn't want to feel like my world was going to end if he turned out to be the devil I thought he was. Because then who did that make me? What sort of person gave themselves to a man like him?

I blinked away the tears and saw that Greyson had left his watch on the floor. I bent down and picked it up, trying to ignore the slight excitement that was bubbling in the pit of my stomach. I had just been with Greyson less than ten minutes ago, but I was already excited to see him again.

I slowly put my clothes on. I didn't care about the other tests. I wasn't going to take them. I had already decided that I was leaving at the end of the day. It seemed odd to me that I'd only been here for a few days. It felt like years. I felt like I'd known Greyson my whole life, but I hadn't even known him a week.

I could feel my head pounding as a headache came on. I placed Greyson's watch in my pocket and walked to his office. I slowly opened the door, but the room was empty. I sighed as I realized that he wasn't there.

I decided to walk to his private living room to see if he was there. As I walked, I thought about the evening Greyson had sung to me and how we had danced around the room. It had reminded me of a scene from a movie. An old romantic movie. A movie where the men were still men and knew how to treat a lady.

I arrived at Greyson's study and paused as I looked through the window. Greyson was lying down on the couch, and he appeared to be reading a book. I stood there and watched him for a few minutes. He looked so peaceful and so handsome. My heart ached for myself and for Greyson. What demons were eating him up inside?

"He's very handsome, isn't he?" Patsy's voice surprised me as she stood next to me. I looked at her with wide eyes, but she wasn't looking at me as she spoke. "He's a wonderful man, Greyson is."

"I don't really know him," I mumbled.

"No, you don't. I've known him a long time." Her voice sounded wistful. "I was his first employee here at the club."

"Oh." I looked at her in surprise. "I didn't know that."

"Why would you?" she said dismissively as she looked at me with a slight sneer.

"You must know a lot of what goes on here?"

"I do." She nodded and stepped back. "I know everything."

"And you still work here?" I asked softly, hoping to get more information.

"Of course I still work here. Greyson knows he can trust me." She made a face. "I love him, you know." She looked back through the window at Greyson. "And love means loving someone no matter who they are."

"Oh." I stared at her carefully then. "I didn't know."

"I've loved him from the beginning. I thought at one point that my love could change him. Or at least save him." She sighed. "You can't help who you love."

"Does he love you?"

"He doesn't do love." She shook her head and then looked at me with a mean expression. "What are you even doing here? You should be in a test room."

"I was just walking around."

"I already told you that could get you in trouble."

"I should get going," I said reluctantly and she nodded.

I walked away quickly and slowed as I rounded the corner. I peeked back and watched as Patsy knocked on the door and entered the room. I quickly returned to the doorway and held my ear up against the door. At first, the sounds were muffled, but I realized that was due to the loud beating of my heart. I took a couple of deep gulps of air to control my breathing and tried listening again.

"Greyson, it's for the best." I could hear Patsy's voice clearly now, and it sounded like she was pleading. "We should leave. We can start over. You know I'll always support you."

"No, Patsy. I'm not going to leave."

"But you have to. She knows what happened and now—"

He cut her off angrily. "How do you know she knows?"

"She told me." Her voice was tight. "And there are others."

"There are others who want to do what?"

"They want to take you down, Greyson." Her voice was frightened. "It's not safe here anymore."

"I don't run from the truth, Patsy. This is my club."

"But, Greyson," she pleaded.

"You need to leave now." His voice was curt.

"Okay." She bit back a sob. "But don't say I didn't warn you. She will be the undoing of you and me."

I ran back around the corridor quickly, opened the door to a room, and slipped in to hide. I watched Patsy leave Greyson's room with a dejected face and tried not to feel emotional.

I couldn't believe that I hadn't realized just how in love with Greyson she was. Did he love her? Had he ever loved her? Had they ever been intimate? I cringed at the thought and ignored the sick feeling that was building up in the pit of my stomach.

I left the room and ran back to Greyson's study. I was about to knock on the door when I realized it was still slightly ajar and he was on a call.

"Brandon, it's Greyson." His voice was smooth as he spoke. I peeked an eye through the opening to spy on him as he talked on the phone. His features looked hard and his body looked tense. "We have a big problem. No, I don't want you coming and bringing your girlfriend with you again." He paused, and I could see him pacing back and forth. "Look, Brandon, I need your advice. We have a Maria problem going on right now."

I fell backwards then and clasped my hand over my mouth. The blood drained from my face as I walked quickly back to my room. Was that the real reason why Maria was dead? Had she found too much information about the club? Had she threatened to tell the police? Had she been murdered? My footsteps increased as a flash of pure worry and fear hit me. Was I going to be the next Maria?

CHAPTER SIX

Greyson
Ten Years Ago

The room was smoky and the lights were dim. The music was pumping at just the right level—high enough to create some excitement but low enough so that the businessmen could relax and chat without feeling like they had to shout. The ambience of the club was spot-on—it reeked of money, sex, and a good time. I should have been happy about that. I had the hottest, most exclusive club in New York, but I wasn't satisfied.

I watched as some of the girls danced in cages on the stage at the front of the room. I watched as a senator walked up to the stage and just stood there gazing at a beautiful Asian girl as she danced her way to the floor. He called over his friend, a man I recognized as a top director from Hollywood, and they stood there watching the girls dancing. They seemed to be entranced by the dancers and waited there for a few minutes before going back to their booth at the side of the room. I watched as Patsy walked over to their table, ready to take their order.

I was pretty sure they wanted the girl from the cage, but those girls couldn't be ordered. They didn't do anything but dance. But I knew that Patsy could still make them happy. We had a bevy of girls who were ready to give lap dances, blowjobs, whatever the men asked for—if the price was right.

"God, it was a mistake to go home with Maria. You were right." Brandon grimaced as he distracted me from my thoughts. "I didn't realize she thought this was serious."

"What did you think it meant when a girl asks you to go home with her?"

"I didn't know her parents and her sister were going to be there. Shit, her little sister basically asked me when we were getting married."

"Did you throw up?" I laughed. "Two whiskeys on the rocks, Denise." I nodded at the girl in front of me.

"Sure thing, Mr. Twining," she purred at me as she bounced her breasts around. I didn't even bother to watch her as she walked away, even though she had the fittest ass I'd ever seen.

"She's pretty hot." Brandon watched her as she walked away, and I groaned.

"Dude, do not date another girl from the club. Do not even fuck them. It's not a good thing."

"How was I to know that Maria would turn out to be a psycho?"

"You know she does coke."

"Coke doesn't make someone a psycho."

"Don't mess with the girls," I said again slowly. "This is already a mess."

"You don't even know the half of it." He sighed and leaned forward. "She said she loves me. She said that she can make things difficult."

"She can't be making threats like that." I jumped up as I saw Denise approaching, grabbed the whiskeys from her tray, and downed them quickly. "Two more." I glanced at her as I put the empty glasses back on her tray.

"Yes, Mr. Twining." She blinked her eyes at me as seductively as she could. I felt her nipples brushing against my arm as she tried to flirt with me. "Would you like anything else?"

"No." I shook my head and made eye contact with her. "Do you like it here?"

"Yes, I love it, Mr. Greyson." She nodded eagerly, and I could see adoration in her eyes.

"It's Twining."

"I meant Mr. Twining." She blushed then, and I could see the terror in her eyes. She was afraid of me. That upset me. I didn't want the girls to be afraid of me. There was nothing to be afraid of. I'd never hurt any of them. Or slept with them. Aside from Patsy, and that had been a mistake. That wasn't to say I was a monk. I had plenty of women. Just women I picked up from outside.

"How old are you, Denise?"

"Twenty, sir."

"Should you be serving alcohol?"

"Don't know." She shrugged. "It doesn't really matter, though. I've been drinking since I was twelve."

"Do you have sex at the club?" I wasn't sure why I asked the question. I'd never really cared about the girls before or who they were or what they did. They just had to look good, dance well, have a pretty or sexy smile, and be up for the job.

"I've had sex with some men, sir." She tried to smile, but it never reached her eyes. "It paid very well."

"Did you enjoy it?" For some reason, her answer was extremely important to me. I'd always been of the thought that women thought of sex like men did. It was fun and it felt good, and it was a bonus if they got a little something out of it.

"It was fine." She looked at the ground and took a step back. I frowned as I stared at her. She didn't look like a woman who was happy with the perks of the job.

"I see. Go and get the whiskeys now."

"Yes, Mr. Twining." She hurried away fast and I went and sat back down with Brandon.

"Do you think the girls like their jobs here?" I asked him casually. He looked up at me in surprise.

"Who knows?" He shrugged. "I'm sure some do."

"Not all though?"

"Who really wants to be a slut or a whore?"

"They're not sluts and whores." I felt annoyed at his choice of words.

"Greyson, half of these girls are on drugs and alcohol so they can sleep with some of these slobs."

"What are you saying?"

"I'm saying, I don't think most of them actually enjoy working here. But we don't care, right?"

"Yeah. We didn't force any of these girls to take the job."

"They got lucky getting a job here," Brandon continued. "Half of these girls don't have any skills. What are they going to do? Most of them were getting high before they even got here. Most were probably sleeping with bums in the street for twenty bucks. We're helping them change their lives."

"Are we really?" We stared at each other for a moment and I knew that we were both feeling as much doubt as each other.

"We can't change it now, Greyson. We're in too deep."

I changed the subject. "What you going to do about Maria?"

"I'll take care of her." He sighed. "I'll shut her up. Make sure she doesn't go spouting her mouth off anymore."

"Good. We don't need her making any trouble."

***

"Hi, want a dance?" A cute tan girl with dark brown curly hair approached me as soon as I entered the deviants room. The deviants room was dark and private. Only men at the highest level of the club were allowed to enter. There were about twenty girls who worked in the deviants room and they all knew that anything went.

"No, I'm okay." I shook my head and continued walking.

"But I'd love to show you a good time." She reached out for my arm and I stopped.

"What's your name?"

"Janice."

"Nice to meet you, Janice."

"It would be nicer if you let me give you a dance."

I stared at her for a moment, at her sweet impish smile, and realized that she must not know who I was. As the thought struck me, I smiled. "Sure, why not."

Janice grinned, grabbed my hand, and pulled me to the side of the room to a black leather couch. "Would you like any particular music?"

"No. Surprise me."

I sat back and concentrated on her, trying to stop myself from looking at what was happening elsewhere in the room, though it was hard. I could hear the sound of the sex swing as it moved back and forth and tried to make a mental note to get someone to come in and oil it. I wondered who was on it and smiled. I knew the sex swing had been a good investment. Who didn't like finding new ways to have sex?

"I'm a sexy, sexy bitch." Janice sang out to me and I watched as she started swinging her hips as she bent down to turn on some music. Her ass was sticking in the air for all to see, with only a small black thong. She was wearing some sort of cowgirl covering on top. It had long leather tassel, but it did a good job of accentuating her large breasts.

She stood up and walked towards me like a model on a catwalk as the music started playing. Her confidence surprised me as she sat in my lap and started her slow dance to a Boyz II Men song. She pushed my chest back so that I was sitting back in the chair and slowly undid her top. She rubbed her nipples in my face as she threw it on the floor, and she started groaning.

"You make me so horny," she whispered into my ear as she ground her ass into my lap.

I started to feel uncomfortable at the spectacle she was making of herself. Is this how she acted every night? It just seemed so fake, and I wasn't feeling turned on at all. I was glad that she didn't know who I was and she was showing me how she treated the patrons of the club. This behavior was not acceptable for the private club. It was too fake and artificial. This might be okay for a cheap dance at a strip club located at a seedy part of town, but it was not okay for an exclusive club.

"Janice, I need to go ..." I started to get up and she pushed me back down.

"But, Mr. Twining, I wanted to thank you for being so nice to my friend Maria."

I looked up at her in surprise. "What?"

"I know that Brandon used her, treated her for a fucking fool. But she said you were nice. You made her feel like she was more than just a piece of meat."

"I don't know what you're talking about."

"Just sit back and enjoy." She smiled at me. "It's been too long."

"What's been too long?" I frowned.

"Since you've had a release." She reached down and massaged my cock through my pants before I pushed her off of me.

"I don't know what you think you're doing, but you're done."

"Don't you like it?" She looked at me in surprise. "I thought you would have liked it."

"You're mistaken. Come with me." I grabbed her arm and escorted her out of the room.

I could tell that some of the other girls had seen us, and they watched us curiously as we left the room. Some of them had jealous looks on their faces. I knew that they were wondering what she had that they didn't. They didn't know that I was about to fire her and not fuck her.

"Janice, this isn't going to work out." I looked at her as we entered my office. "I'm afraid I'm going to have to fire you. I don't think you're a good fit for the club."

"What?" Her eyes widened and then grew small. "But I need this job."

"I'm sorry." I shrugged. "I'm sure you'll find another one. You're a very pretty girl."

"I can't believe this." She sat on the chair in front of me. "Let me have another chance, please."

She walked over to me and looked into my eyes for a second before reaching up and undoing my zipper. She pulled my cock out, and before I knew what was happening, her lips were on me and she was bobbing up and down. I groaned as she started sucking me off and closed my eyes. I hadn't expected her to try and convince me in this way.

***

"Greyson, you need to come right now." Brandon's voice sounded panicked on the phone.

"What's going on? Where are you?" I yawned as I stretched in the bed.

I froze as I realized that I had company. I looked over and saw Janice cuddled up next to me. I wanted to slap myself. I couldn't believe that I had slept with her. It went against my policy of getting involved with the women in the club.

"Greyson, it's Maria. Please just come."

"Where are you?"

"Maria's room."

"Why are you in Maria's room?" I sighed and looked at the clock on my bedside table. "It's fucking four a.m., Brandon."

"Just fucking come now. I'll tell you when you get here." Brandon's voice sounded strange, and he hung up the phone.

I stretched once more and rolled out of bed.

"Where are you going, honey?" Janice smiled up at me through closed eyes and I shuddered at her endearment.

"I'm not your honey," I muttered. "I'd like you to be gone by the time I get back."

"What?" Her eyes flew open then and she sat up. Her breasts sat high on her chest and I realized that they must be fake.

"You heard me." I sighed. "Please be gone by the time I get back."

"So that's it." She looked hurt. "What about—"

"What about nothing, Janice. I don't want anything from you or with you. This was a mistake."

"I see." She bit her lower lip. "I thought that—"

"Be gone by the time I get back." I pulled on some jeans and a shirt and strode out of the room.

I walked through the corridors quickly, trying not to think about all the questions and worries rolling around in my mind. The club was eerily quiet as I walked. Nothing much happened at four a.m. Even the men who had participated in kinky sex were usually fast asleep at this hour.

I walked past the doors of the room that I knew contained the dungeons for the more adventurous and couldn't stop the feeling of shame from sweeping over my body. I stopped in the hallway for a few seconds as I tried to control my breathing. I wasn't happy with what the private club had become. It wasn't that it was so different from my initial expectations of what we wanted at the club. It was just that it felt wrong.

I started to wonder if in some way I hadn't been exploiting women who were too weak to do anything about it. As I'd grown older, I'd mellowed out a bit and forgotten the heartbreaks and aches of my childhood. I no longer despised or judged my father. I no longer hated my mother for dying. I no longer ridiculed women who wanted to sleep with me right away and let me know it. The fact was that a lot of the emotions that had made me who I was today no longer existed inside of me. As I'd grown older and the club had become more successful, the more I felt like maybe I'd taken the wrong path.

My ringing phone interrupted my thoughts.

"Greyson, where the fuck are you?" Brandon's breathing was odd as he yelled into the phone.

"I'll be there in a minute. Chill the fuck out. What is it? Is Maria pregnant?" I muttered into the phone and hung up as I rounded the corner to the hallway of the girls' rooms. I saw the open door and walked in slowly.

"Okay, I'm here. What's going on?" I strode in, feeling irritated and annoyed. Brandon's face looked back at me with an ashen expression.

"I'm so sorry, Greyson." His pupils were dilated, and I followed his gaze to the bed.

My heart stopped for a few seconds as I saw a lifeless Maria lying on the sheets naked. There was blood on her pillow and her body looked like it was blue. I walked over to her quickly, not even conscious of what I was doing. I picked up her wrist and tried to feel for a pulse.

"It's no use." Brandon's voice broke. "She's dead. Maria is dead."

CHAPTER SEVEN

Meg

Present Day

I quickly ran down the hallways. I needed to find David. Even though I didn't really like him, I knew he would be able to help as an undercover cop. I felt scared. I didn't really know what to think about anything anymore. It seemed to me that Maria might have been killed because of what she knew about the club. And from the way it was looking, there was a long list of suspects.

What scared me even more than that was the fact that I could be the next Maria—or maybe Nancy was the next Maria. I knew from David's comments and the worry in his eyes earlier that he definitely knew Nancy and that he was concerned about her disappearance as well.

I made my way to the courtyard to see if he was still there, but it was empty. I paused for a second, trying to still my panic and think. Where could David be? What could he be doing? If I were David, I would be looking for Nancy. And if I were an undercover cop, I would be looking for clues. And the first place I would look for clues would be in her room.

I started running again, and this time I tried to think of what I was going to say when I saw him. For some reason, I didn't want him to know everything I knew. I ran to my room and pushed open the door. I nearly sank to my knees in relief as I saw David standing there.

"Hey." I watched as he jumped back from my bed. "What are you doing?" I frowned at him.

"I was searching the room to see what happened to Nancy." He looked at me angrily and I saw him pushing something into his pocket.

"What the fuck, David? Are those my panties?" I walked towards him. "What sort of a sicko are you?"

"Oh, it's okay for Greyson to have the goods, but not me?" He retorted back at me and I stopped.

"Excuse me?"

"You think I don't know you're fucking Greyson every opportunity that you get?" He looked disgusted. "Even in the pool? What a slut you are."

"It was you in the room?"

"Yes. I came to talk to you. See if you knew anything about Nancy, but you were too busy having fun with the boss."

"What I do is none of your business."

"I guess you chose him over me because he has more money." David reached out to touch me and I flinched.

"Don't touch me, David." I glared at him. "And for the record, I would never be with a man like you. Greyson's money doesn't mean anything to me."

"He'd flip if he knew we fucked." David's glance grew ominous. "It would be the perfect revenge."

"Revenge for what?" I swallowed hard and took a step back.

"It wouldn't just be about revenge. I really do want to fuck you. You're sexy as hell."

"Leave me alone, David."

"When you call out my name, I want you to say Ryan. I want you to scream, 'Fuck me harder, Ryan!'" David was almost panting, and I looked around the room for an object I could use as a weapon if he tried to assault me.

"Wait, what did you say?" I froze and stared at him for a moment as my brain comprehended what he had just said. "Why do you want me to call you Ryan?" And why did that name sound familiar to me? I didn't know any Ryans.

"That's my name." He shrugged. "My real name."

"Ryan." I looked at him again and then it hit me. "Maria's ex-boyfriend was named Ryan."

It was his turn to freeze then. His eyes grew cold and he surveyed me. "How did you know that?"

"So you did know Nancy, then." I nodded to myself. "Nancy is Maria's sister and you were her ex-boyfriend."

"I was her boyfriend." His voice cracked. "She said she was coming to New York to be an actress. We were still together. She didn't even dump me. We were still officially dating when she brought that jerk home."

"That was Brandon, though. Not Greyson."

"Everyone knows that Greyson's the real mastermind here at the club. Nothing would have happened if it wasn't for him."

"So you joined the police force to investigate him?"

"No." He laughed at me and gave me a pitiful stare. "I'm not in the police force, Meg. That was a lie to gain your confidence."

"So why are you here then?"

"I wanted to find out what happened to Maria. I want to know how she really died." His voice choked. "I wanted to get revenge."

"So why did you get Nancy to come?"

"I'm pretty sure that they are trafficking women. Too many women disappear from here on a weekly basis. I needed someone on the inside who could testify for me. Nancy was going to be that girl."

"So where is she?"

"That's what I don't know." I could see the fear in his eyes. "We argued and then she was gone."

"What did you argue about?" I asked him.

"You."

I was taken aback. "Me?"

"She told me to leave you alone. She told me that she didn't want to see you hurt."

"I don't understand."

"I was going to make you fall for me. That was why I came and kissed you. I was going to seduce you and make you want me." His eyes studied my body. "It wasn't all about revenge, you know. I do think you're hot."

"Thanks." I rolled my eyes, trying not to shudder. I couldn't believe he was so cocky as to think I would actually want to be with him. That I would ever choose him over Greyson. Never in a million years. They didn't even compare to each other.

"She told me to leave you out of it. I told her it was the best way to get back at Greyson."

"How would that be getting back at Greyson?"

David laughed. "He loves you."

"No, he doesn't." My heart skipped a beat. "I don't even know him."

"Trust me, he loves you. Maybe he doesn't even know it yet. But you forget, I've been here for two years. Greyson doesn't even interact with the girls once they start. He hasn't been able to keep his hands or his eyes away from you."

"It's just sexual attraction."

"Who knows? How does it feel to be the devil's mistress?"

"He's not the devil," I whispered.

"He's going to burn in hell." David's eyes flashed. "I'm going to make him pay for what happened to Maria."

"Shouldn't we find out where Nancy is first?"

"I could take you right now and it would kill him." He grabbed my wrists and pushed me up against the wall. "He'd never be able to look at you the same way again, knowing I made you come and scream my name." He laughed as he kissed my neck. "I know, you see. I know what it's like to lose someone I love and know she's fucked another man."

"It's not Greyson's fault that Maria left you, Ryan."

"He started this fucking club. He uses women for his own gain. If it weren't for him, she never would have met Brandon. Brandon didn't even love her. I loved her. I still love her!" He banged his fist against the wall. "I wanted to marry her. Do you understand that? I wanted to marry her and start a family. I loved her so much. I just let her go to New York to try and make it. I always thought she would come back to me. Instead, she came back with a coke habit and a new man."

"Coke habit?" I frowned. "She was a drug addict?"

"Not when she left!" he shouted, and his hand gripped my neck. "When she left, she was my beautiful, innocent Maria. When she came back, she was a different person."

"Please, David—I mean Ryan—you're hurting me!" I gasped and tried to push him off of me.

"Do you think I haven't been hurt?" His eyes were red as they looked into mine. "They killed her, Meg. I need to get my revenge."

"But what about Nancy?" I squeaked, barely able to breathe. "If you kill me, we may never find her."

"Why did she have to go and disappear?" He groaned and released his hold for a second. I kneed him in the groin and pushed him back hard. "What the fuck?"

"Leave me alone!" I screamed. "Leave me alone and I will help you find Nancy!"

Ryan looked at me then with a contemplative look. "I want to hurt you." His voice sounded pained. "I want to hurt Greyson. I want to make him pay."

"Brandon is the one who dated her, Ryan," I said softly.

"But Greyson is the reason for all of this." He clenched his fists.

"You can still take down Greyson," I mumbled, ignoring the hole in my heart. "Let's try and find Nancy first."

"How?"

"Let me go and see Greyson. Let me try and find out what happened to Nancy."

"I don't trust you." He shook his head. "You'll tell him."

"Nancy is my friend." I shook my head. "Her safety is my number one concern."

He looked at me thoughtfully then. "Okay." He nodded. "We can still fuck if you want."

I looked away from him then and bit my lower lip to stop myself from screaming again and crying. "Let me go and find Greyson now."

"Don't take too long." His voice issued a warning. "I'll be here waiting."

"Okay." I exited the room quickly, my heart beating fast.

I didn't know what to think or to feel. I walked numbly and made a side trip to the bathroom, where I promptly threw up. I felt sick to my stomach as I sat there trying to calm myself down.

"You can do this, Meg."

I jumped back up and splashed some water on my face. I stared at my reflection in the mirror and studied my face. I looked like a different person. I could see it in the new lines of my face. There was something more mature in my expression.

I walked out of the restroom slowly. I was scared that I was about to find out that Greyson was just as bad as I'd imagined. I knew that I was going to leave the club. There wasn't going to be another night for me at the club. I knew that I was going to be scarred for the rest of my life by this experience. I didn't want to prolong the agony anymore. I'd still try and find Nancy, but I wasn't going to do it from the club.

I made my way to Greyson's office and slowly opened the door. I peeked in and saw him sitting at his table, writing something on a piece of paper. My heart stilled as I gazed at him working. He didn't look like the sort of man who could cause so much pain and heartache. I studied his features, trying to memorize his face for the future. This is how I wanted to remember him.

He looked up then and gave me a broad smile. "Meg, come in."

"How did you know I was here?" I pushed open the door and walked in.

"I always know when you're around." He stood up and walked towards me. "It's like a sixth sense."

"Funny." I smiled weakly, not sure how to say what I wanted to.

"I was just writing something." He nodded towards the table.

"Oh?"

"But I can share it with you later." He put his arms around my waist and pulled me towards him. "It's good to see you. I've missed you."

"Sure you have." I didn't want to take his words at face value, but it was hard not to be happy at his words.

"I have." He kissed me softly on the lips. "You don't even know."

"No, I guess I don't." I sighed as I kissed him back. I felt my body melt into him, loving the warmth and comfort his arms provided.

There was nothing that felt as good as being embraced by Greyson. But I couldn't stop thinking about Ryan and his hands around my neck I couldn't get the image of the pain in his eyes out of my mind. Ryan was a crazy psychopath, but he had loved Maria. He had really loved her. And he had lost her because of the club. Maria had died because of Brandon and Greyson and the club. I knew that for a fact. I just didn't know how she died. I instinctively knew that whatever had happened wasn't at Greyson's hands. He was a lot of things, but he wasn't a murderer. I knew that from the pits of my heart and soul. Greyson Twining was many things, but he wasn't a killer.

"What's wrong, Meg? You seem sad." His gaze changed as he stared at me.

"Make love to me, Greyson." I leaned up and kissed him. "I want you to make sweet, passionate love to me."

"You do?" He grinned.

"Yes." I nodded. I wanted one last lovemaking session with him so that I could remember every detail of it.

"You can't get enough of me, can you?" He swung me around and laughed. He put me down and ran his hands through his hair. "We'll go to my room."

"Your study?"

"No, my bedroom." He grabbed my hand. "I want you to see my bedroom."

"Okay."

I followed him until we got to a small room in a side of the club I'd never been to. He took out a key, opened a door, and led me in. I gasped as I looked around the room. It was beautiful and full of light. There was a big king-sized bed with grey sheets and a large cream shag rug next to it. It was very masculine but very welcoming.

"I love it."

"I love you," he said softly and I froze.

"What did you say?" I blinked up at him and he stared back at me with a shocked expression.

"Nothing." He shook his head and turned around. "Let me get some wine."

He walked away from me and I stared after him, wondering if I had heard correctly. Greyson walked back with two wine glasses and a bottle of wine and sat on the bed.

"Join me." He called me over and I walked to the bed and sat next to him.

"This is different." I made small talk as I waited for him to open the bottle.

"You wanted different, right?"

"I'm surprised you're not telling me that I should be begging you right now."

"I don't need you to beg." He handed me a glass and put the bottle down on the ground.

"Really?"

"I'm a changed man." He laughed, and I stared at him to see if he was being serious.

"Sure you are."

"Brandon really loves Katie." He looked at me seriously. "I've never seen him like that before."

"Does that make up for his sins?"

"He's not perfect. But are any of us?"

"Katie doesn't deserve to be hurt and used."

"He wouldn't hurt her."

"Not as badly as he hurt Maria, right?"

"You know, when I met Brandon, he was a different guy," Greyson said slowly. "He was the guy that I wish I had been. He had the values and the right ideas."

"So what happened?"

"I happened." Greyson lay back on the bed. "And I always wonder what would be different now if I hadn't happened."

"Do you wish anything was different?"

"I wish everything was different." His eyes connected with mine for a few seconds. "I wish that everything was different." I saw pain in his eyes then and my heart broke for both of us.

Greyson was a man broken by his past and perhaps even his present. He was a man filled with regrets that were eating him alive. I put my glass down on the ground, moved up the bed, and took his face in my hands.

"You can always change your future, Greyson." I leaned down and kissed him tenderly. I pressed down on his lips and allowed my tongue to lick them slowly. I wanted to taste every small piece of him. I wanted to consume him. I wanted him to know that this was special. I wanted him to remember this for the rest of his life.

Greyson stared at me as I kissed him and I sat on him gently.

"Are you okay?" I whispered as I lifted my head slightly.

He nodded at me and I bent down again to kiss him. This time, he kissed me back. His lips were moist and eager, and I fell down on top of him as his hands wrapped around me. My tongue eagerly entered his mouth and his tongue met mine with just as much vigor. They danced together in slow motion as his fingers worked their way up my back and into my hair. He rolled me over onto my back and gazed down at me.

"I've never been better in my life." His words sounded thoughtful, but I didn't have time to respond before he kissed me again.

This time, his lips were rough and his hands roved my body as if seeking salvation from my every skin cell. We both sat up and pulled our clothes off, not even thinking about what we were doing. Both of us just needed to be together. We were both broken, and it was as if our bodies together made us feel whole again. We completed each other. He made me feel more alive than I'd ever felt before. His lips kissed my cheek and then down my neck. They didn't stop moving until they came to my right breast and he proceeded to bite my nipple. My fingers scratched his back as he teased me, and I pushed him back so that I could get on top of him again. I looked down at his laughing eyes.

"I like a woman who likes to take control."

"Shhh." I placed my finger on his lips. "This is my turn."

I proceeded to kiss his lips and then his cheek, making my way down to his chest, licking his nipples lightly and then biting on them hard. I could feel his breathing speed up and I grinned as I continued kissing down his body until I got to his abs. I ran my fingers across his stomach and moaned as I felt his cock move against me encouragingly.

"In its own time, Greyson." I laughed. And then I continued on my journey.

I took him into my mouth, gently at first, licking him as I would an ice cream cone I wanted to savor. Then I increased my pace. He tasted salty and sweet at the same time, and I sucked him eagerly. I felt him still and his fingers gripped my hair and pulled roughly. It hurt a little bit, but it only intensified the feelings of lust that were coursing through my body. My fingers gently rubbed his chest hairs as I continued sucking him off, and I knew that he was moments away from coming.

"Stop," he whispered and pulled me up. "I don't want to come in your mouth."

"I don't mind."

"You're the first girl I've ever had in here. I want it to be special." He rolled me over to my back again. "I want to watch your face as I make you climax."

I lay back as he slowly lowered his boy on top of mine.

"Just give me a second." He grinned wickedly. "If I enter you now, I'll come within seconds."

"I don't mind," I said again.

"No, I don't want to come until I hear you panting." His fingers played with my hair. "I don't want to come until I feel you coming all over my cock."

"You're so rom—" I started but gasped as I felt his fingers gently rubbing my clit. "Oh, Greyson."

"Oh, Meg." He grinned back at me. "Cat got your tongue?" He winked as he slipped a finger inside of me. I closed my eyes and tried to stop my body from trembling as I felt a second finger entering me. "You're going to be the undoing of me."

"No," I moaned. "I, oh my!" I screamed as soon as I felt his tongue licking me and his lips descended on my clit. "Oh my ..." My legs clutched his head between my legs. "Greyson."

"I lied," he whispered. "You *are* the undoing of me." He pulled up and within seconds he was inside of me, moving slowly so that I could feel every inch of him as he entered me. "You were the undoing of me as soon as you walked through those gates."

"The pearly gates of hell," I moaned as I writhed against him.

Greyson grabbed my hands and increased his pace. My breasts bounced against his chest, and I wrapped my legs around his waist so that I could feel him deeper inside of me. Greyson groaned as my hands squeezed his ass and I started gyrating my hips underneath him. We moved in beautiful symphony as our bodies built up to their final release. I knew the second it was going to happen for both of us, as we both stilled for one second before our bodies started moving frantically, anticipating our sweet releases. We held on to each other tightly as we came, and our lips sought each other as our orgasms took over our bodies and connected us as one.

***

"Your body is so warm after lovemaking, and it glows." He stared at me wonderingly. "Did you know that?"

"I didn't." I smiled at him, exhausted but wanting some answers.

"I love just being with you." He pulled me closer to him and held me tightly.

"Greyson, will you tell me what happened to Maria, please?" I leaned back and stared at him.

He closed his eyes and sighed. "Why do you want to know?"

"It's important."

"She died."

"How did she die, Greyson?" My fingers traced the lines on his face as I tried to memorize his features.

"You don't want to know." He shook his head and he opened his eyes again. They looked at me bleakly. "You really don't want to know, Meg."

"Do you know where Nancy is?" I prodded.

"No." He looked away from me and then his phone started ringing. He reached down and picked it up. "Greyson."

"Greyson, it's Patsy. Mr. Stephanopolous is here to pick up the girls." I closed my eyes and pretended that I wasn't listening to the conversation.

"Okay?"

"One of the girls is refusing to go." Patsy sounded stressed through the phone.

"Tell her that her life will be better this way." Greyson sighed. "Take care of it, Patsy."

"Yes, Greyson." She hung up and he looked up at me.

"I suppose you heard that."

I nodded, too choked up to say anything. It was true then. It was confirmed. Greyson was in the human trafficking business.

CHAPTER EIGHT

Greyson

A Few Days Ago

The *résumé* in my hands didn't make sense to me. Why would a lawyer apply for a bartending job? Or a job she thought was bartending? She didn't fit the profile of the girls I hired to work at the club. A lawyer would only mean snooping and trouble, but I was curious as to why she was here. What sort of woman went to two interviews for a job that had to cry out as being not very legitimate? Not a woman with any sense.

"Your next appointment is waiting in the hallway," Maggie said through the phone to me. "Though I don't know if she's right for the club, Mr. Twining."

"Why's that, Maggie?"

"She wanted to know your name." She continued. "They never want to know your name."

"Thanks, Maggie." I hung up the phone and sat back.

It was possible, of course, that she was a journalist trying to find out what was going on at the club. Though this would be an odd way to go about it. I would think she'd pretend to have been a dancer in her previous life, not a lawyer.

I stood up with an odd feeling in my stomach. I felt excited about seeing who this girl was. Her *résumé* didn't have her name on it, which I thought was odd. I walked to the door, opened it, and looked outside into the dark hallway.

My breath caught as I stared at the beautiful redhead sitting waiting for me. She had an air of confidence about her that I wasn't used to seeing at the club. She didn't look like a lawyer, though—not with the sexy outfit she had on.

"You here for the interview?" I asked her roughly. I was angry at myself for feeling drawn to her. I always prided myself on my complete and utter lack of feelings. It was how I had gotten so far.

"Um, yes," she squeaked, jumped up, and walked over to me. Her dress was even shorter than I'd thought, and I stared at her legs as she made her way towards me. She looked like sex on legs. I shifted as I stood there staring at her, surprised that I was already starting to grow hard.

"What's your name?" I barked at her, annoyed with myself. I should just send her away. Every nerve in me was shouting that this woman was trouble and that she did not belong at the club.

"Jada." She swallowed and I stared at her long, graceful neck. I tried to hide my smile as she lied. There was no way that this girl's name was Jada. No way at all.

I invited her into the room with me and we made small talk. I wasn't really sure what she was saying. I was too caught up in her heaving breasts as they teased me from the top of her dress.

I shifted in my chair uncomfortably as I stared at her *résumé*. This woman was different from every other woman I had ever met. I wasn't sure how I knew that or why I knew it. But instinctively, I knew.

"Take your clothes off," I commanded, trying to gain control of the situation and my mind. I needed to think of her as every other girl.

"What?" Her jaw fell open as she screeched. Her eyes looked at me in shock, and I tried not to laugh. She definitely was not private club material.

"I said, take your clothes off." I stared at her impatiently. "Now," I demanded, curious to see what she was going to do.

"I heard you." She glared at me, and I missed the rest of her words as I watched her eyes sparking anger at me.

She was angry and shocked, and she wasn't hiding her emotions from me. I found myself liking how strong she was. In this business, I very rarely came across strong women. I knew then that I had to tell her to leave. I didn't want to find myself liking her. I was about to tell her to leave when my phone rang.

"This is Greyson Twining," I answered while still staring at her face. She was beautiful even while she stared at me with contempt.

"Greyson, it's Brandon." I stilled as I heard his voice. It had been a long time since we'd spoken, and I was surprised to hear his voice.

"Listen, there is a girl coming to interview at the club. Her name is Meg. She's a cute blonde. Do not hire her. Whatever you do, please do not hire her."

"I don't know what you're talking about, Brandon. You can't tell me who I can and can't hire." I was annoyed at his call but noticed that the girl in front of me had started looking at the ground. I stared at the top of her head and could see a slip of blond at the front. She was wearing a wig! "No cute blondes named Meg have come in today. I gotta go." I hung up then, suddenly curious as to how she knew Brandon and why she was here.

I stood up and walked closer to her. I could see her looking at me with a confused expression. I stared back at her and grinned inwardly as I saw her staring at me body and take a step back. She looked back up at me and I could see the desire in her eyes. It made me happy.

I leaned towards her and she closed her eyes, eagerly awaiting a kiss. I pulled her wig off and laughed lightly as she opened her eyes slowly. There was disappointment in them, and I knew then that I had to have her. Her face was so expressive and her eyes told me everything she was thinking. I wasn't going to turn her away.

I didn't know how she knew Brandon and I didn't care. I didn't even care that she might be the demise of the private club. All I knew was that I had to have her. I had to get to know this wonderful, mysterious girl. Even if it changed everything in my life. Especially if it changed everything.

***

It had only been two days, but everything in my life felt different. Suddenly the sky seemed bluer and the grass seemed greener. Even the sounds of the birds chirping had become a melody I didn't want to stop. And it was all because of her.

It scared me how Meg now occupied my mind. How her body made me feel. How she made me feel. I felt like a new man. Everything in my life had changed the day Maria died. My whole world had come crashing down and I hadn't known which way was up. I felt responsible for her death even though I hadn't been the one to pull the trigger. She had died because of a series of events that I had put into motion.

Ever since that day, I'd been trying to seek redemption for my sins. But I'd known that whatever I did wouldn't be enough. I'd never be enough. My life was never going to be more than it was.

But then she arrived and everything changed. I found myself opening up to her. I was drawn to her like a moth to a flame, and she was drawn to me. I tried to warn her to stay away. I knew that I would end up hurting her as well. But I'd rather she hurt because of my rejection than because of the real me. I wouldn't be able to stand to see the look in her eyes when she realized who I was.

I wasn't proud of myself. I tried to warn her. But I just couldn't step away from her. I didn't want her to leave, yet I needed her to leave. Meg Riley was going to be the undoing of me and it scared the hell out of me.

I opened the files on my desk and looked at the files of all the girls I'd sent away. There had to have been at least five hundred girls that had gone through the club now. Five hundred girls, yet it wasn't enough.

"Greyson?" Patsy knocked on the door and then walked in. "Are you busy?"

"No, come in." I looked up at her and smiled.

I felt ashamed for the way I had treated Patsy. She had been loyal from day one even though I had treated her like shit. We'd slept together for about a week when she'd first started and then I'd just stopped wanting to be with her. I hadn't liked the fact that she had seemed to be falling for me, so I'd allowed her to walk in on me fucking another girl. It had seemed easier than telling her that 1 hadn't wanted her anymore. She'd never complained or screamed. She'd just accepted it and kept working for me. And now she was one of the only people who knew that went on at the club. She knew everything.

"I wanted to see how you're doing."

"I'm fine. Why?"

"You've seemed different." She shrugged. "More antsy."

"I'm fine."

"You can leave this all behind you know, Greyson." She walked up to the desk. "We could leave, let someone else take over. You don't have to do this anymore."

"I can't stop now." I shook my head. "This is my bed. I need to lie in it."

"No, you don't," she countered. "This doesn't have to be your life."

"Patsy, is there anything else?" I sighed and looked at her expectantly. I didn't want to be rude and throw her out of the office, but I was getting annoyed.

"I thought you didn't believe in love." She bit her lip and stared at me. "I thought that the reason you were the way you were was because you couldn't love."

"I don't know what you're talking about."

"But you're different. You care about that Riley girl, don't you?" Her eyes looked sad. "I wondered why you hired her. She doesn't fit the mold of the girls we accept at the club. Not the old club or the new club."

"Patsy," I started, but she shook her head.

"No." She sounded upset. "I just wished I understood what she has that I don't. I've seen it all, Greyson. I know who you were and who you are and I'm still here."

"I know and I appreciate that."

"I'm still here. I've always been here. I've kept your secrets, but you still don't love me."

"I don't love anyone." I sighed, not even knowing how I felt any more.

"You don't see it yet, but I do. We all do." She turned away from me. "But she'll destroy everything, Greyson. She won't be able to accept it. I know girls like her. She doesn't know what life is like. The real grit, the dirt, the hard times, the bad times, the evil times. She doesn't know it like I do. She's not worth your energy, Greyson."

"Please don't talk about her like that," I said softly, trying to hide the anger building up in me. "Please, Patsy."

"You don't even know her!" Her voice rose. "How can you feel this way about her already? I've been here for years."

"Patsy." I sighed. "I'm sorry. I don't know what to say."

"She's going to bring it all back up, you know. That girl Nancy? She came to me, but I don't know where she went. She's Maria's sister, you know."

"I know." I nodded. "I know a lot of things, Patsy."

"Oh?" She looked at me then and her face stilled.

"I know about you and David."

"What?" Her eyes popped open. "I never told him anything, I swear."

"I know, Patsy. I trust you." I walked over to her and hugged her. "I trust you and I love you like a sister, Patsy. But I don't love you as anything more. I will never love you like that."

She didn't answer then, but I could feel wet tears on my shoulder as she sobbed. I held her tight, sad that I had broken her in this way. I felt sick to my stomach. It seemed that all I did was bring pain to women.

I allowed her to get it out. But as I stood there, all I could think about was Meg. My beautiful, wonderful Meg. I knew that she had questions about the club. She had questions and she had theories. I was scared to tell her the truth while she still had some hope about me. I knew that once she knew the truth she would be gone and I'd never see her again. And I wasn't ready for that to happen just yet.

I wasn't ready for the heart I hadn't even known existed until a few days ago to break already.

CHAPTER NINE

Meg

Present Day

I walked through the corridors aimlessly. I felt empty inside. The phone call had changed something in me. It had made me completely raw inside. As soon as Greyson had received another call from Patsy, he'd had to leave. He had asked me to wait so we could talk, but I'd slipped out of the bedroom as soon as he'd left. As far as I was concerned, I needed to get out of the club.

I didn't want to see Ryan again and I didn't want to be around Greyson any longer. I could no longer play the ignorance game. He was evil—pure evil. Maybe there was some good in him that was aching to break out, but I couldn't be that woman who would wait and see if it was going to happen.

I rounded the corner where the nursery was and stopped suddenly. The door was slightly ajar, and I walked up to it carefully to peek in. I saw that there was a baby in one of the cribs and the room was filled with some people. I recognized Patsy and Greyson but there was a man and a girl I didn't recognize.

"She said she won't go without the baby." Patsy sounded annoyed.

"Jessica, you have to go." Brandon stroked her shoulder.

"I don't want to go without my baby." The girl shook her head and started crying.

"I will make sure they take care of you." The other man spoke up. "This is for the best of you and your baby."

"But I don't want to go."

"You have to go." Patsy stood in front of her. "They are waiting for you, Jessica. They've been waiting for a week."

"But my baby!" the girl cried and then the baby started wailing.

"We will take care of your baby." Greyson rubbed his forehead. "You have my word."

"But what about me?"

"You'll be taken good care of."

"That's what you tell all the girls."

"Well, it's true." Greyson looked annoyed. "I have to go."

"But, Greyson—" Patsy reached out to stop him and he pushed her away.

"Take care of this, Patsy." He strode towards the door and I backed away fast so that he didn't see me.

I ran quickly to his office as I knew that that was the way out. My heart was beating so quickly that I thought I was going to have a heart attack. I reached the hallway where I had sat outside on that first day and stumbled and fell to the ground in tears. I could barely see where I was going. I jumped back up, dried my eyes, and took a deep breath. I had to get out of this place and I had to leave now.

I ran through the entrance to the gates and was just about to leave when I froze. I knew that he was behind me, even though he hadn't said a word.

I turned around slowly and stared at him. He looked at me wordlessly and stayed still. He didn't move towards me and I didn't move towards him. We just stared at each other in silence. His face looked remote and closed off, and I knew he could tell that I'd been crying.

He finally spoke. "Were you going to leave without saying goodbye?"

"I didn't think it was needed." I shrugged and looked away.

"You were just in my arms a few minutes ago." His eyes questioned me.

"You left me to go and send someone else away." My voice broke and he frowned.

"What are you talking about?"

"I saw you with the girl and the baby."

"Oh." He ran his hands through his hair. "That's my business, Meg."

"I can't believe you can stand there and say that so calmly!" I shouted, angry now. "As if it's no big deal." I walked towards him now. "You can't just treat women like that. It's not right."

"I told you I'm not a good man."

"I didn't want to believe you."

"You should have believed me." He sighed and took a step towards me. "Brandon was always the weaker one."

"So? What does that have to do with anything?"

"That's why I told you and Katie that everything was my fault."

"Huh?"

"In the club. Maria's death. Everything. I take responsibility for it all."

"It is your fault." I paused. "Or are you saying it's not really your fault?"

"I wanted Katie to believe it was all me." His eyes drilled into mine. "I wanted to absolve Brandon in her eyes."

"Are you saying it wasn't all you? Is Brandon still involved with the trafficking?"

"What?" He frowned. "No, I don't know what you're talking about."

"Then explain it to me."

"Will you come back inside?"

"No." I shook my head. "Tell me now. Tell me here."

"When we started the club, I was a spoiled, cocky rich boy. I wanted to own the world. I wanted to provide a club for the richest men in the world to enjoy. Part of that enjoyment came from women."

"Prostitutes?"

"No. Yes. I don't know." He sighed. "The lines are blurred. The women knew what they were getting into and none of them had to do anything they weren't comfortable with."

"I see." I looked away as a heavy feeling filled me.

"The club grew quickly. All the richest men in New York wanted to join the club. Then we got businessmen from LA, London, China—all over the world."

"I see."

"Word spread that we had the most exclusive club in the world. But no one knew exactly what was going on. We had so many different rooms and so many different levels, and each level had access to something different."

"So men paid to have sex with women."

"Essentially, yes," he sighed. "I'm not proud of myself or what the club became, Meg. Every day, I wish that I hadn't started the club."

"Sure."

"The day that Maria died was the pinnacle of all my bad days. I'd been starting to regret what the club had become, but it was that day that I realized that it needed to end."

"What happened to her?" I looked at him with worried eyes. I was scared that he was going to tell me something terrible.

"She shot herself in the head." His eyes were wide with pain, and I took his hands into mine. "She called Brandon right before she did it. He walked into her room a few minutes after it happened."

"Are you sure it was her?" I asked, unconvinced.

"Yes." He nodded. "She left a note and the police verified that the gunshot was self-inflicted."

"Oh my God." My eyes widened. "Why did she kill herself?"

"She thought she was in love with Brandon. He rejected her. She got high on drugs, saw him with another girl, and I guess that was it."

"That's awful." I stared up at him. "Absolutely awful."

"I told Brandon not to mess with the girls, but he never knew how dangerous it could be. Neither of us really knew how damaged most of the girls who worked at the club were. We had a lot of drug addicts, former prostitutes, runaways, abused girls."

"That's horrible."

"Yes." He nodded sadly. "It broke us both when she killed herself. Brandon left the club right away. He blamed himself for what happened. He didn't want anything to do with me or the club."

"He couldn't have known she would kill herself." I sighed. "That's horrible. Why did he tell Katie she was his college girlfriend though?" I frowned. "That doesn't make sense."

"You'd have to ask him." He shrugged. "I don't know much about his life after he left, aside from an incident he had with Denise and a couple other girls we fired a few years later."

"Denise?" I looked at him blankly.

"She was a girl who worked at the club." He sighed. "But it doesn't matter. That's not my story to tell."

"So what happened after Maria killed herself?"

"I closed the club immediately. We refunded all the yearly dues, and I tried to think what I could do to make amends."

"What happened to the girls?"

"They freaked out. They made good money at the club, even though they hated it. Brandon and I pooled together and gave each woman who went to rehab a million dollars upon successful completion."

"Wow. That's a lot of money."

"We made a lot of money." He shrugged. "Neither Brandon nor I have ever experienced a life without a lot of money."

"That must be nice."

"Not really. You don't notice or appreciate it when you're born with it." His eyes looked away from me. "So do you hate me yet?"

"No." I shook my head. "I don't hate you."

"I hated myself when I realized what the club stood for. The subjugation of women. It made me realize that I'd gotten it all wrong. Women weren't in it to hurt us. At least most women weren't. They wanted to uplift their men. Most women just wanted to love and be loved. But they had issues just like us. And many of their issues were caused by men. I realized that I needed to help to uplift women who had been damaged and were on the wrong path. The club attracted all the women who needed our help the most, but instead we just hurt them even more."

"I guess with your childhood, you didn't really—" I started but stopped as he put up his hand.

"That's not an excuse." He shook his head. "Do you know how many women I've met who have been on drugs since they were kids because they wanted to forget the pain they couldn't get out of their heads? The pain of being abused by their fathers or their uncles. The hunger that they'd lived through for years that selling their body for ten dollars seemed like a good option. Women who had nothing and did anything and everything they could to get a meal or a warm bed for the night."

"It's not your fault that they grew up like that."

"But I didn't do anything to help. If anything, I further used them." His voice broke. "My club was the epitome of everything wrong in our world."

"So what did you do?"

"I decided to try and help these women." He stared at me hard then, and I could hear the determination in his voice. "I knew that we got a lot of women applying to work at the club that had problems, so I decided to let that work for me. We continued advertising and hiring girls. Only this time, we weren't hiring them to work at the club. We were hiring them to see how we could help them."

"Help them?" I was confused.

"We send the girls to different rehab houses, Meg." His voice was strong. "Alcohol, drugs, vocational school, new-mother training. Anything we think can help improve their lives."

"What?" I frowned.

"That's why we do the tests. We're not looking to see what skills you have for working in the club. We're looking to see your weaknesses and proclivities. If you go for the cocaine or the heroin in the drug room, we know that we need to get you to a drug rehab right away."

"I didn't even see the heroin."

"That's because you're not a drug addict." He smiled at me and squeezed your hand.

"What about the spelling test? What rehab do you go to for that?"

"We send the girls to different schools with tutors. The spelling test and the math test are to see what level they fit in so we know better where to send them."

"Oh." My eyes widened. "So you're not sending them to men."

"To men?"

"Like as sex slaves?" I muttered quietly, feeling like a fool as I said it.

"No, of course not." He frowned. "I would never do that, Meg. Never."

"What about the babies?"

"Some girls come to us when they are pregnant. We have a nursery that we set up to help look after the babies while the women get clean."

"Oh, that's nice."

"We don't want there to be any excuse to stop them from getting clean."

"I can't believe you do all that."

"I wish I could do more." He sighed. "I wish I could help every woman who needs it."

"It must cost you a lot of money."

"Money doesn't mean anything to me."

"Does Brandon know that you send the girls to rehab?"

"Yes." He nodded. "He helps to pay the bills."

"Oh?" I was shocked.

"Yeah. His company, Marathon Corporation, donates $100 million to the club every year."

"Wow."

"He's a good guy." He kissed my cheek. "He's a really good guy. If it weren't for me, he always would have been a good guy."

"You didn't make him do anything, Greyson." I pulled his face down to mine and kissed him. It was then that I noticed that there were tears on his skin. "Oh, Greyson." I reached up and wiped them off of his face. "Are you okay?"

"I'm fine." He kissed me back. "I just expected you to pull away from me and leave."

"I didn't know the truth." I shook my head. "I thought you were really evil and I hated myself for still wanting to be with you. I didn't know who you really were."

"You do know who I am. I'm a dark bastard." His fingers gripped my arms. "I don't blame you if you hate me."

"Oh, Greyson. I could never hate you. Please never think that. Greyson, look at me." I pulled his face to look at me. "You are a wonderful human being."

"I hurt women, Meg. I'm responsible for someone killing herself."

"No, no, you aren't. Neither you nor Brandon is responsible for Maria's death." I kissed him again. "Please get that thought out of your mind. Greyson, this club was every man's fantasy, and while I don't like the sound of it, that isn't what this club is now. You're helping people. You are changing lives. Hundreds of lives. You're a good man, Greyson. You went through the fire and you came out on the other side."

"I never would have believed that if it weren't for you." He stroked my cheek. "You've made me believe that there could be salvation for me. You've made me believe that tomorrow could be a brand-new day, a brand-new me, in a brand-new life."

"Greyson, I think that we were meant to meet." I wrapped my arms around his waist. "I think we were destined to change each other's lives."

"Where do we go from here?" He cocked his head and looked at me.

"I don't know." I pressed my head against his chest and listened to his heartbeat. I wanted to tell him all of the things I held deep in my heart, but I knew it was too soon. We didn't know each other that well, and both of us were still too fragile from everything we'd been through.

"We can figure it out." He kissed the top of my head. "Would it sound crazy if I told you I loved you?" he whispered, and my heart started racing as I looked up at him.

"Yes, it would sound very crazy." I shook my head and giggled. "You don't know me well enough to know if you love me."

"My heart knew I loved you as soon as I saw you." He grinned down at me.

"Your heart is silly." I couldn't stop myself from grinning back at him.

"This wasn't how I imagined this going." He raised an eyebrow at me. "I've never told a woman I loved her before."

"Do you really want to hear me tell you I love you?" I cocked my head. "Won't that scare you away?"

"You could never scare me away."

"Then yes, Greyson Twining. I love you. I love you from the tips of my toes to the hair on top of my head. And I think we're both crazy."

"That's why we're perfect for each other." He held me tight to him.

"We have to take this one day at a time." I stared up at him. "I've seen what happens when people rush things. I don't want us to rush this. I want us to do this right."

"I will do whatever you want me to, Meg. Whatever, whenever. I'll even leave the club if you want me to."

"No. I want to help you here." I squeezed his hand. "What you're doing is wonderful. And I don't know why you're so secretive about it."

"I don't want people praising me for doing good like I'm some sort of choirboy. I'm not that good. I'm just trying to seek forgiveness for all the bad I've done."

"I understand, and that's why I love you." I kissed him again and he kissed me back passionately. "There's just one last thing."

"Yes, my dear?"

"Do you know what happened to Nancy?"

"No." He shook his head. "I have no idea."

"We need to find her, Greyson. I'm worried something happened to her."

"We'll find her, my love. I promise."

I stood back and stared up at his handsome face, unable to believe that I had ever doubted him and who he was. I could see the love and slight insecurity in his eyes as he gazed back at me. I would never get tired of staring into his blue eyes. This was a man I felt I could spend the rest of my life with. This was a man whom I knew would never knowingly hurt me.

We stood there just holding hands, and I smiled to myself at how lucky I was. I looked up and stared at the private club. I'd had no idea that this place would bring me such joy when I'd first arrived.

A small motion at one of the windows made me pause. I glanced up and saw David and Patsy standing at one of the windows, looking down at me and Greyson, and I froze. I gripped Greyson's hand and turned away.

I was pretty sure that there was a lot more going on at the club than Greyson even knew about. And I was determined that I was going to get to the bottom of it all. But first I needed to find Nancy. I had a feeling that she knew a lot more than she had let on before she disappeared.

"What are you thinking about?" Greyson's hands fell to my ass.

"I think the more important thing is what are you thinking about?"

"I think you know the answer to that." He laughed and his mouth kissed my neck.

I closed my eyes and let myself enjoy the feel of him next to me and against me. I felt safe in Greyson's arms. I knew he would protect me and love me, just as I would protect and love him.

An image of a little Greyson running around crossed my mind, but I kept my thoughts to myself as I giggled. *One step at a time, Meg. One step at a time.*

AUTHOR'S NOTE

Thank you for reading *The Private Club* series. If you enjoyed the series, please leave a review.

There will be a follow-up series called *The Love Trials* starting in April 2014 that will focus on Nancy and the other secrets at *The Private Club*.

There is also a sequel coming out called *After The Ex Games* that provides insight into Brandon, Katie, Greyson, and Meg's lives. *After The Ex Games* and *The Private Club* Serials.

Please join my mailing list to be notified as soon as new books are released and to receive teasers: http://jscooperauthor.com/mail-list. You can find links and information about all my books here: http://jscooperauthor.com/books. I also love to interact with readers on my Facebook page: https://www.facebook.com/J.S.Cooperauthor.

As always, I love to here from new and old fans, please feel free to email me at any time at jscooperauthor@gmail.com.

ABOUT THE AUTHOR

J. S. Cooper was born in London, England and moved to Florida her last year of high school. After completing law school at the University of Iowa (from the sunshine to cold) she moved to Los Angeles to work for a Literacy non profit as an Americorp Vista. She then moved to New York to study the History of Education at Columbia University and took a job at a workers rights non profit upon graduation.

She enjoys long walks on the beach (or short), hot musicians, dogs, reading (duh) and lots of drama filled TV Shows.

Made in the USA
San Bernardino, CA
19 October 2014